WICKED TALES
FOR
WICKED PEOPLE

BRENT ABELL

SAD House Press

Wicked Tales for Wicked People

WICKED TALES FOR WICKED PEOPLE

SAD House Press

Introduction

I am a lucky man. Over the past three years I've been able do what I love doing, writing. It started out on a lark, but it has grown. What began as something to do for a laugh turned into something I want to do as a career. In your hands is the beginning of my journey, the genesis of my dreams. Some of the stories contained in this book are very early and show a writer trying to find his voice. The later work is from a writer who is still learning the craft (do we ever really stop learning?) and has found a good stride. A few of the tales are from out-of-print and hard-to-find anthologies and others are from eZines. I have also included four new stories.

Why do a collection now?

I've heard from a few people that trying to get some of the older anthologies is hard and expensive. I haven't included all of the old stories, but I held onto them for a reason. Most of the stories have been given small updating and some of the old voice cleaned up a little. The idea of a collection has been floating in my head for some time and with work on the novels and novellas moving forward, I felt the time was just right. Some of my favorite author's books have been collections and I hope this one gives everyone a favorite story or two they'll go back and read over and over again.

As always, I want to thank my family for their support and their love. Without my wife, sons, and megalomaniac pug I'm not sure where I'd be now. To all the publishers who gave the stories in this book a chance, I thank you. Lastly, to all the

3

friends I've made in the author world, thanks for all the support and advice.

Brent Abell

TEARS OF HEAVEN

"Mommy, why is Daddy crying again?" Gail whispered, leaning over to her mother.

"Daddy's had it rough, baby. After everything that happened, he's just had a tough time getting through it," Melinda answered, running her long, thin fingers through her daughter's honey blonde hair. She let go of the bangs and wrapped Gail up in a tight embrace. Gail buried her face against her mother's slender shoulder and let out a small whimper.

A faint, sweet-smelling breeze blew through the park and Melinda used her thumb to wipe the solitary tear from her daughter's eye. Around them, children played and other people strolled by laughing and talking. Some stopped to check on the sad pair in each other's embrace, but in the end they all passed them by. Mother and daughter gave each other another big squeeze and turned back to observe Doug.

***

Doug sat perched on the edge of the bed, elbows propped up on his knees, his face cradled in the palm of his hands. Light sobs and sniffs escaped his mouth and nose. Salty tears formed a pool in his hands and drained away, dripping onto the stained carpeted floor. Doug shook and raised his head. Wiping his damp hands on his dirty, ragged sweat pants, he took a long, deep breath, and opened his eyes.

The room still looked the same as it did before, a godforsaken shit hole where people went to escape from life or to finally give up and die. A small lamp in the corner, *sans* lampshade, threw out a dim spot of light in the dark room. Cockroaches darted out from under the bed and found cover beneath the chipped and faded nightstand against the wall where the clock blinked the same time. Snow hissed on the old television screen, calling out for the plug to be pulled. The dingy motel room looked more depressed then Doug felt. When he hit rock bottom, he hit it hard. Thinking about it, it didn't really hit him as much as it kicked him in the balls while simultaneously sucker punching him in the face.

Groaning, Doug went to the bathroom, and when he returned, he sat back down behind the beaten desk beside the old television. The pen and paper still lay there, mocking him. Every time he tried to write something, the words flowed through his mind, burned through his arm, but stopped short of transferring onto the paper from his fingertips. Doug didn't know writing a suicide note could be so difficult.

***

Sitting slouched in the plastic-coated chair; the past year swam around his head. The last drops of bourbon ran down his throat and landed in his stomach with a welcome burn. It had been days since he'd eaten, and without any food to absorb the alcohol, it roiled his insides and he felt bile race back up his throat.

Humph, how much better am I, always drunk and ready to die? I'm a poet and didn't know it! He thought with an ironic chuckle.

Since Melinda and Gail were killed coming home from ballet class one night by that worthless, drunken, sack of shit

Eli Jacobs, Doug failed to see a reason to continue living. Every day when he looked up to the sky, he hoped they were happy wherever their souls might be. He hoped they couldn't see him unravel while he drank himself into oblivion, unable to put their memory to rest. If God did exist and Heaven is where good, innocent folks went when they died, he wanted God to spare them the pain of watching him fail to come to grips with what happened and lose himself in the never-ending litany of booze and drugs. If He let them witness his downward spiral, He, too, was a son-of-a-bitch. Gathering his thoughts again, he placed pen to the paper and finally began to write.

To anybody that cares (or whoever finds my body),

My name is Doug Clark. I am a widowed man who buried my wife and only baby girl at the same time. I looked to God for an answer, for a reason. All I found was the bottle. I can't go on any longer; I want to be with them where ever they are. Heaven, Hell, I don't care. I'm sorry for the mess; I left extra cash on the bed to cover it.

Sincerely,

Douglas James Clark

Sighing, he reread the note and wadded it up. Tossing it in the air, it bounced off the other dozen or so attempts overflowing from the trash can. Like everything else in the last year, he failed, again. Snatching up the bottle and remembering he emptied it earlier, he smashed it down on the desk. The clear glass shattered and showered the floor.

He cried out and hung his head down, his body shaking from the force of his sobs. The loss and sadness cloaked him as he drifted off to sleep in a haze of booze and pity.

***

"Melinda, I wish you wouldn't bring Gail here to witness this tragedy. Doug is a mess and I hate to think what she thinks of her father now," the man said, sitting down on the bench next to them. The garden surrounding them was silent and he pointed to a box sitting in the middle of the cobblestone path. When a person strolled by, they kept their distance and passed without even a glance to the families gazing into their boxes. The men with the hoods stayed to the right of the path, respecting Melinda and Gail's need for privacy during their visitation.

"Hank, I love him and I want her to see how much he misses us. I don't want him to hurt, but it shows how much he loved us," Melinda muttered.

"He's my son, my blood, and the greatest joy in my life. Don't you think I ache on the inside watching him spiral out of control? That boy was all I had in the years after my lovely Jackie passed on. We missed her and seeing him down there like this after your death tears at me here." He pounded his chest above his heart.

"I wish I could have met her, she meant so much to both of you," Melinda said with a sigh.

"I loved her so, but there's nothing you can do while still in the flesh on Earth to change things," Hank shrugged.

"How long do we have to wait?" Gail said, reaching out to her grandfather.

"You know the rules, sweetie-pie," Hank replied. "He's not ready to join us yet." He smoothed Gail's golden hair.

"I want to hug my daddy!" "She yelled and wiggled free from Hank's grasp.

"No honey, don't!" he called after her. Jumping up, he hurried to stop her from reaching the box.

Gail ran over to the box and looked in. Her father looked so small and helpless. Closing her eyes, she pictured herself in the doll house-like box, hugging her daddy. Drawing a deep breath, she focused long enough for her body to dissipate into a mist and her essence to seep into the box.

Diving toward his granddaughter, Hank reached out to grab hold of her before she faded away into the box to save her father, but his fingers passed through her arm as she dissipated. Hitting his knees, he felt the world unravel around him.

He knew all was lost.

***

Sitting back down at the desk, Doug picked up the gun and stared at it again. The .45 felt cold in his hands, even as his palms broke out into a sweat. The rush swelled in him and he stuck the barrel in his mouth again. Slowly, he closed his lips and bit down on the gun. The steel tasted tangy and the oil bitter. Hesitation settled in again. Doug dropped the gun from his lips and inhaled deeply. His breath caught in his chest, sensing something wasn't quite right. The curtain fluttered as though stirred by a breeze. He knew the air was off because it didn't work and hadn't since his first night here.

Glancing around, he felt the air grow cool and the hairs on his neck and arms rose until they pointed to the ceiling. On his right, a groaning bed spring cried out in the silent room.

Cautiously turning his head, he noticed the indention in the center of the bed. It disappeared and the sweet sound of a child's laughter lightly called across the room. A loud pounding, like running, circled around him and he swung his head from side to side trying to follow the sounds. After a few trips in the circle, the room fell silent once more.

The fleeting scent of his daughter's lilac bath soap filled his nostrils. Doug reached out and swept his hands wildly through the air, trying to grasp anything in the empty space surrounding him, hoping that something would touch him back. His open palm touched something cool in the air beside him. His hand stopped and he held it perfectly still for a moment, picturing Melinda and Gail.

Flashes shot through his mind like an old movie, memories of the life he had shared with his family. Crying out from the sharp pain, memories continued to flood through his brain. Each moment of his life became a pricking in his soul while fleeting images of his wife and little girl filled him. As suddenly as it began, the sensation disappeared and the loneliness crashed back down around him.

Then he felt something wet splash on the back of his hand.

A small liquid drop, the size of a tear, ran down to his wrist, and then fell from his flesh. On its downward journey the drop vanished into nothingness before hitting the floor. Curious, he touched his tongue to the spot where the drop touched his hand and an electric jolt shot through his body, burning every fiber of his being as he consumed the salty residue.

Like a flower on a frigid, frosty morning, what little hope remained within him withered and died. The darkness he embraced during the past year consumed him in one last bleak wave and his reasons for living vanished without a trace. With a new-found conviction, Doug picked up the gun again. In his heart he felt ready to do the only thing that made sense to him.

Quickly, he placed the gun back in the upright position, put up the tray table, and smiled. Doug sucked on the barrel twice in anticipation, and when the gun's seed exploded into his skull, his parting thoughts were about being with his family again.

***

Melinda cried out and Hank flinched, both watching Doug's head splash on the grimy yellow hotel wall in a crimson spray of brain, blood, and bone. In horror, Melinda looked away as the cockroach popped out from under the bed and danced through her husband's gray matter.

"No, no, no! It wasn't supposed to be like this," Hank muttered, shaking his head.

Melinda turned to him, "What do you mean 'supposed to be'?"

"He told me everything would be alright if we believed and followed the rules." Hank shook his head, trying to deny the reality of what he had just witnessed.

"Who Hank?"

"*Him*, all we had to do was believe," he answered pointing to the sky. "He willed us to be together when Doug finished his journey. It wasn't going to be like this, Gail ruined everything. She violated the laws. She made contact! Now, she's doomed us!"

"What do you mean about Gail? What did she do, Hank?" Melinda frantically screamed at him. Rushing over, she pounded her fists into his big barrel chest, sobbing with each hit.

Reaching out, he grabbed her wrists and drew her to him. He placed a finger on her trembling lips to silence her. He let her go and led Melinda to the box to see the damage Gail had caused.

On the floor and walls of the box that looked like a motel room, the pulpy chunks of Doug's head slid around through the skin and hair to stitch itself together again. Soon, all the bits and pieces shook and started reforming Doug's ruined face. The crimson wall faded back to its normal dirty shade and the bullet sprang from the wall and disappeared in the gun's chamber.

Covering her mouth in startled realization, Melinda turned away, unable to watch any longer.

***

Doug opened his eyes and wiped the sleep from his tired eyelids. The cockroach ran past his foot and slid behind the TV stand, disappearing from sight. Looking over at the table, he saw the gun staring back at him. He got out of bed, sat down at the desk, and began writing his suicide note for the fourth time in an hour.

With slumped shoulders, he opened the curtains and looked out on a dead world and wondered where everybody had gone.

Seven hours later, after he felt his daughter's spirit with him, he pulled the trigger to join them.

***

Doug opened his eyes and wiped the drool from his chin. He did a double-take when the cockroach skidded across the floor and hid in the dark recesses of the dirty motel room. A sense of déjà vu danced in his thoughts. He got up and gazed out the window at the grey morning. The sun sat buried behind the clouds and the smog blanketed the city, a typical Los Angeles morning. On the freeway, nothing moved. He didn't see a car speed by for several minutes.

Maybe it's Sunday and everyone's still in bed, he thought and closed the smoke-stained curtains. Sitting back down, he put pen to paper and began to write his last words.

Seven hours later, believing his daughter had come to lead him away, he put the gun in his mouth. The bullet slammed through Doug's head and painted the wall in the pinks and reds of blood and brain matter.

***

Doug opened his eyes…

***

"Hell is repetition my dear," Hank whispered to Melinda.

Gail sat behind the bench under the weeping willow tree, her knees pulled up to her head, tears rolling down her cheeks.

"I made a deal to release him from his netherworld prison, but his physical contact with Gail broke the arrangement."

"What arrangement?" Melinda asked. She tried to hide the tone in her voice, but her anger, fueled by the pain of her husband's grisly end, only continued to grow.

"His suicide on the mortal plane left his soul in jeopardy for a millennia. All he had to do was redeem himself in Purgatory for a shorter time, now he is doomed to repeat the act in Hell for eternity. I have to pay my price now also. I laid my soul on the line to save him, and now my bill is due. Please, for Gail's sake, don't try the same thing. Leave us be and look after her."

Melinda turned and looked at him, "What price are you talking about?"

"Wailing and gnashing of teeth is my forever and ever, like my son now. I bet my soul that Doug could save himself. When Gail touched him and he tasted her tear, he felt her spirit and gave up. She made him want to die so he could be with you again. Now, I've got my own box as my reward."

One of the hooded figures bent over and placed an empty box on the path next to Doug's. Turning toward Hank, the figure bowed and walked away chanting. Inside the box, the blankness swirled and forms started to take shape.

Hank stood before them and screamed. Smoke poured from underneath his shirt and pant legs. His searing flesh popped and blistered as the flames licked up from the stone pathway, consuming his immortal body. He called out one last time before he fell to a pile of ash on the cobblestone walkway. The ashes swirled and blew around until the remains of Hank funneled into the box on the ground.

Melinda and Gail peered inside the box as Doug blew his head all over the wall again. Hank's remains reformed in the new box that appeared besides his son's prison and screamed at his personal Hell.

***

Seven hours later, Doug took up the pistol once again to end his life, while in the next box Hank reached out and failed to stop Gail from entering her father's tormented prison. A cloaked man stopped on the path in front of Melinda and Gail. Beneath the hood, Gail saw him smile at her and she gave a faint little wave in return. Afraid of the strange man, she grasped onto Melinda's leg and turned away.

The figure bent over and picked up the two boxes. He blew them off and placed them on the wall next to the pathway and continued on his way. The veil fell away from the wall and Melinda saw the rows of clear boxes stacked on top of each other reaching high into the eternally blue sky. Gail cautiously approached the wall and glanced in the boxes at eye level. A person sat in each box she peeked in. Most of them looked like a loop on the television, replaying the same scene over and over again. Cries and screams of agony echoed along the wall of boxes, each one a prison for some doomed soul.

Melinda walked over and gazed in on Doug and Hank one last time before turning and walking away, hand in hand with Gail, toward the gold cityscape in the west.

As mother and daughter strolled off into the cityscape's golden spires, Doug pulled the trigger… again, and Hank ran after Gail… again, over and over.

Father and son, side by side, bound forever in repetition.

***

STORY NOTES:

Hell is repetition… at least that's what they say and I wanted to explore the theme with this story. For some reason, I was feeling really twisted and wondered what a man would go through if he relived his suicide over and over again. Not feeling twisted enough; I threw in his dead wife and daughter having to witness it too. Like some of my work, this one touches lightly on religious themes and in this case I poke a little at Purgatory. One review of the story spoke to the world-building I did with the wall and the depiction of Heaven I used, but honestly, it was a one-time deal. If I do come back to it at some point, it will be in a novella trilogy I have started to plot out for the next year or so.

SPOT SHOOT

For the tenth time in the last hour, Carl fired a quick barrage of gunshots out his attic window at the shapes lurking below. Every time he peered out to survey the lawn, another zombie tried to hide in the bushes or make their way up the front walk toward the door. Louise was dead and gone twice now and he hadn't heard from his only son Dale since the mess started. Like clockwork, he awoke every morning, checked the perimeter from the second story windows, and then he would try to relax because it hurt like hell to even move. This is what his life was reduced to in the new world, the world after they came back and wouldn't stay dead.

Over the past two months, the war between the living and the dead raged around him; and he was running out of bullets. When the dead started walking, he didn't have time to hit the sporting goods store during the chaos of the normal world screaming to a halt. Nobody really knew the how's or why's of the dead returning to life, everybody just knew it happened. By the time the news outlets caught wind of how wide spread the problem was, the networks were crashing and the radios were going off-air into static and then a haunting silence. Information was as scarce as supplies in the world. His food stores were depleted three days ago and he was glad his thirst vanished overnight.

Carl cocked his head over towards the remains of his wife. There were still small tatters of flesh hanging off her bones and her wedding band had slipped from her skeletal finger onto the floor. He had eaten the rest of Louise earlier in the morning with a splash of ketchup and some pickle relish; if not for taste then he did it to cover up the discoloration the skin and muscles had taken on. The body remained in the kitchen where she died, he'd brought the hand up to munch on while keeping watch on the lawn. The fetid flesh still tasted bad, but he didn't care, his belly eagerly accepted it. He put the ring on his pinky and it fit. A few weeks ago it wouldn't have, so he knew he must be losing weight. He hit his fingers together and heard the rings cling in the quiet kitchen. Her ring was the last piece of her he had left now.

Since the bowels of hell opened wide and the dead came spilling forth, existence was done on a day to day basis. He always thought the book of Revelations amounted to complete and utter bullshit, but now he figured the Jesus freaks were right.

Sometimes it really sucks to be wrong, he thought to himself and fired another shot down below.

He'd be fine as long as he didn't get bit by one. The shit from the movies was something else that surprised him: a bite would turn you, flesh tasted good, and a blunt force trauma of some sort to the head would kill you.

Why the hell am I always wrong about everything? He mused.

The day passed with only a few more rounds fired below. The sun started to set in the west and exhaustion began to overcome him. Carl knew it was getting to be time to begin his nightly ritual. He let out a grunt as his stiff joints groaned while he began to bring himself to his knees. He gingerly pulled himself up to his feet and used the rifle to steady his shaky body before trying to walk. Carl carefully went to each door and window, checked the boards he'd nailed in place to keep unwanted things out, and then retreated back to the attic where he would continue his assault on the living dead. Taking his shooter's position, he watched the day fade into night.

***

He snapped awake and was instantly upset at himself for dozing off. The sounds of footsteps pounding on his back sidewalk brought him back to the war whether he wanted to be back in it or not. He shouldered his rifle and slowly positioned himself so he could see out of the window. Following some sudden movement in his scope, he scanned the bushes and found the shadows of three shapes moving around the yard. Carl carefully flicked the safety off and gently put his finger on the trigger. His stomach rumbled.

He drew a bead on the front shape and squeezed the trigger. The explosion of the bullet firing from the gun and escaping into the night pleased him. As his stomach rumbled again, he heard the shriek of the zombies as the bullet found its mark. In a bright crimson spray, the bushes were colored in gore and gray matter. He looked through the scope and sighted the brains and skull pieces sliding down from the leaves and pooling on the ground. The two other shapes fled. He wondered if the zombies ever ran like that in the beginning. In the past few days, it seemed they all ran when he opened fired. He compared to the first week when they just shuffled along and never looked like they were much of a hurry to get anywhere. Another yell came from below and for a moment, Carl thought it sounded like Dale, but then it grew quiet outside again.

Exhausted and hungry, Carl slipped into sleep once more and in his dreams he could hear the voices all around him call him home. He'd hoped to hear Dale's voice once more in his dreams, but his voice remained silent.

***

The sun was not yet rising in the east when something jerked him from sleep. A loud clatter sounded from his garage. The banging echoed through the early morning dawn and stopped as quickly as it started. He sat up and groaned again. Getting old sucked and he hated sitting still in one place for too long because his joints and muscles would tighten up. Setting his rifle in the window sill, he pointed the muzzle at the garage and placed his eye into the scope. Someone, or something, had turned the lights on in his sacred garage, his temple. The house had no basement so the garage was his personal man-space, and right now it was being violated.

Carl brought the rifle up and used the scope to take a peek into the garage window. His spot shoot trophies were blocking his view. The numerous awards were for his skill with his rifle shooting. He never shot at an animal, but paper deer and targets feared him and Dale when they went competing in local spot shoots. Dale was a good kid, but he was never the man that Carl thought he should be. While he was smart, Dale was not an expert at sports, fixing things, or fishing.

But boy, that kid could shot though, Carl thought after some effort.

He was able to see enough of the shadows in the garage to make out that there were five of them this time. Looking in the chamber of the rifle, he found only four bullets. It was less than what he thought he had.

Carl hated being wrong… again.

***

Time passed by, and Carl knew the sun would be coming up soon. He also knew the zombies still hadn't left his garage. Once again, hunger pangs raged in his gut. Before long, he would have to make a move, with no food ammo; his days in the house were quickly becoming numbered. The zombies in the garage perplexed him.

What were they waiting for?

The dead didn't have a sense of patience as far as he'd witnessed. Anytime one or more stumbled onto his property, they immediately came to the front door trying to get in.

Why did they go to the back this time?

Waiting for them to come out was making him crazy, but Carl sat motionless, wondering. The stomach growl reared its ugly head again. He had to move. He'd always had his escape planned out in his mind.

"Game on," he whispered and gave his wife one last mournful glance.

Carl slowly stood up and slinging the rifle on his shoulder, headed down the stairs. As he came and passed the pictures in the hallway, he glanced at the memories of a simpler time, with no zombies, and Louise by his side. He tried to cry, but the time that passed had hardened him, he guessed, because the tears never came. He also looked longingly at the pictures of their son, and he wondered if Dale lived or if he wandered around looking for human flesh. He hoped their time spent at spot shoots or out practicing on the range prepared him to handle the zombie infestation. Carl finished making his way down the stairs and shuffled through the kitchen towards the door.

In the back door he had left a small opening he could shoot through if the zombies ever decided to move in on him while he was on the ground floor. He found the wood block covering the shooter's hole and pulled it out. He glanced over his shoulder again at Louise's remains rotting in the corner behind the table. Curious that there was not a smell he could detect, Carl figured he was used to it at this point in time and it was now just a normal part of his senses. The sight made his hunger grow and it sickened him to his core. He tried to throw up but found that he couldn't, the bile never even leaving his stomach. Carl decided it was time to take out the zombie trash once and for all and get out of the house. He slipped off Louise's ring and held it tight and gripped his rifle.

***

Carl waited for what seemed like hours for the zombies to make their move on the house. He had not seen or heard anything else from the garage, but he knew that they were still inside. Nothing had entered or left since they woke him up last night. His arm ached from holding the gun in the ready position for so long and the tightening of his old joints and bones were murdering him. But like a true man, he held his ground and waited… and waited… and waited.

When the sun moved to the central point in the heavens, Carl finally saw movement in the garage. They were finally going to launch their attack on him and his house. He opened the door and took a different shooting spot low on the back porch. He went down to one knee and prepared to fire. From the corner of his eye, he saw one of them move off to the back of the garage like they were going to flank him and then move in. He never moved the gun from the door. Tightening his finger on the trigger he fired off two shots at the garage door. Both splintered the wood and hit nothing else. Carl was left with only two rounds.

The one trying to flank him moved to his right and Carl turned. With his attention focused to the right, a shot rang out from the left. Carl never saw the shot as the bullet ripped through his head. His brain and bits of skull showered the door and the house. Blood sprayed in a wide radius and ran from the gaping hole in his cranium. Five figures stepped out from behind the garage and the corner of the house. They met at the bottom of the porch steps, surveying the corpse, guns at the ready.

"I'm so sorry Dale, but that was a hell of a shot," the oldest looking one said. He placed a hand and squeezed his shoulder as the man started weeping.

"It... needed t-to be d-done," Dale managed to say between sobs. He continued, "W-when I saw he ate mom, I-I knew he had turned. I've never seen one go on about like they were still alive, it was like he didn't even know. R-rest in peace dad."

Dale walked up to the body of his father and closed the eye that remained open in his father's head. Glancing down at Carl's hand, he watched as a ring rolled from his father's dead grasp and fell still by his foot. Dale reached over and picked it up. He held it in the air and turned it back and forth.

"Hey, what do you make of this? My dad was carrying my mother's wedding band," Dale pointed out as he stood up. "He would have started carrying it after he turned, before we arrived the other day."

"I've never seen anything like it. It's like he knew what those represented," answered one of the other men.

Dale reached over and took his father's ring off. Gently, he placed both rings in his pocket and patted it. Bending over, he grabbed his father's rifle, slung it on his back, and the group of five headed back out to fight the undead hordes.

***

STORY NOTES:

What if the world had gone to Hell and the undead walked? What if you had to kill your wife and use her to survive? "Spot Shoot" is about Carl and how he tries to live out his days in his home after the zombies begin to walk. This is another early story and was my second published piece. The interesting thing about this story that will always stand out in my mind is I had somebody wag their finger in my face and get mad at me for the ending. Of course, I also had some who the end went straight over their head. I didn't intend for the ending to be as tragic for Carl and Dale, but when I got to a certain point it had to happen like it did.

GIVER

The black masses dotting the x-ray say it all, I'm dying. And by the sizes of those things, I'm just about done.

I know the doctor tried to make it sound like I had a chance, but I know better.

I've told all who I've helped they were going to be ok. I looked them in the eyes and I alleviated their fear. Did they feel better at the time? Yeah, they felt better and they were cancer free. Sitting here now, staring at my oncologist, I feel the scream welling up from deep within me.

Really kind of poetic, I'm being eaten by the disease I've spent most of my adult life fighting against. I suppose if I believed in a religion I could blame karma or God for turning on me the way my cells have, but I only have myself to blame on this one. Dozens of good turns deserve something other than this doesn't it?

I helped them though, I helped those who sought me out to survive and now the price is mine to pay.

"Brent, are you sure you're ok?" I hear Dr. Wilson Frank say to me. I try to focus on his voice, to show him I understand, but all I can muster is a slight nod.

"I can't... I can't even begin to, I don't know Wilson, I thought I'd be ok like grandpa always was."

"But you're not Brent."

I stand and he reaches out, grabbing my arm and stopping me before I can begin walking away. I turn to face him and I look deep into his eyes and my reflection gazes back at me.

"Look, we can fight this Brent. We have options," I hear him say, but the words mean nothing to me now.

"No, we can't fight it. The method of attacking the cells is gone, I'm spent. The well's gone dry."

"Brent, we have to try."

"I don't want to, I've had a good run and now I just want to cash my chips in and go home."

He looks at me and I can see sadness in his returned gaze. I want to tell him I'll be fine, but he probably would dismiss any words I speak that weren't about the pain I'm in. Right now, a fire burns through my veins and my body feels like I've been set ablaze. I expect to look down at my arm and watch my flesh sizzle and blister. Instead, it's the same pale skin and freckles. In fact, I believe I've turned a duller shade of whitish-gray.

Dying sucks.

"I'll be back next week and we can run the tests again," I say and close the office behind me. Standing out in the cold November evening, all I want is a drink.

***

I try to watch a movie, but knowing I only have a few days left really puts a damper on things. Not even the rum and cola in my hand can bring me the joy it once did and this is probably the most shocking and depressing development of all. Still, I cringe and think back to the ones who are better because of me. I remember being bitten by a dog when I was five and its teeth didn't hurt near as bad as the cancer eating my insides. Shit, I'd take a hundred of those dogs stripping my bones clean compared to what I have to endure right now.

I take another sip and think. Thinking back to how I used my gift, I tear through my memories and everything my grandmother told me about what I could do. Growing up, I knew what my grandfather could do and that gene was passed to me. Right now, I can see his eyes closed forever in the casket. I can still feel the kiss of his dead flesh as I touched his cheek and wept.

I've followed him to the grave before my time.

I've fallen because of his curse.

But, I think I found a way out...

***

Vera Strange thinks she's alone, but I can hear her breathe I'm so close. The late night news covers the sound of my sneakers as I creep through her house in the dark. I watch her sit there and even though she is cancer free, she hacks and wheezes with each breath she takes. She doesn't deserve to keep going. I should have seen it when I cured her. I should have seen how useless she is. What made me think saving an old woman was honorable or right? I'm young and have more to give than her.

I should survive.

The television clicks off and she rises from her chair. Slowly, she shuffles toward her room. I'll give her a few minutes before I go and do what needs to be done. The hallway amplifies the sound of her toilet flushing and the sink turning on. Why can't the old bitch lie down and go to bed?

Finally, the bathroom is silent and I see the light extinguish in her room. Carefully, I move through the hall and crawl through her open door. I try to stay quiet, but the pain is unbearable. Cringing, I moan as a wave of nausea crashes through me.

"Who's there?" I hear her ask and shot up in her bed.

I force the pain back in my mind and try to hold my breath. She rolls around on her bed and the lamp clicks on flooding the room in its soft glow. Its light shines right on me.

"Brent?" she sounds shocked.

"Sorry Vera, I needed to talk to you," I say in a smooth calming tone. I have to stay calm so she can be calm.

"If it's about what you did for me, I thank you. After watching the way my Glenn died of the cancer, I didn't want the pain."

"I know, that's why I took it from you."

Steady. I stand up and I look at her sitting in her bed. Tears dot the corner of her eyes and I feel pity for her. She doesn't deserve what I'm about to do, but on the flipside I don't deserve it either. She reaches out for me and I take her hand. It feels cool and fragile in my grip. I draw her closer and I wipe a tear away. I smile and lean in close.

Her eyes widen as I suck at the air in front of her face. She struggles and tries to pull away as I breathe in the life I gave her. The golden mist hangs in the air between us and I see realization cross her face. Inhaling deeply, I take back in what is rightfully mine.

Vera starts to convulse and I release her. Her body crumples to the bed and I gasp trying to catch my own breath. I stare down at her body and she starts to shake uncontrollably. Small black lumps burst from her flesh and cover her forearm. Her eyes turn a milky white and her chest heaves in short bursts. The cancer is catching up for lost time I suppose.

Better her than me.

Her breathing turns shallow and she sounds like a dying fish. Lung cancer is a bitch. Her body goes still and I watch her take her last labored breath. I close my eyes and the pain subsides. Part of my death sentence has been commuted, my execution delayed. I can feel the cancer begin to lose its fight with me and start regressing.

My idea worked.

Now, I must go down my list and hunt down the others who received my gift and reverse what's been done to me. I have to get the pieces of my life back.

Vera's eyes stare at me in death, accusing me of killing her. I guess in a way I did kill her, but all I did was let nature take its course. Is it any better that my death means she lives? I'm only setting the natural order straight and returning balance to our destinies. Still, I feel sorry for her. I took her life away, but I needed my life back. Reaching down, I close her eyes and walk away.

Looking down at the list of addresses I jotted down, I turn and leave.

I have work to do.

***

"Ah, Brent, please come in and have a seat," Dr. Frank motions for me to enter his office.

The nurse hands him a thick file and she retreats back to her desk leaving the two of us alone. Wilson sits down and flips through the files. Every few seconds, he'd flip a page and glance up at me before continuing to the next page.

"Your test results came back negative. Since we met last week there has been a change. Brent, your cancer free," he states flatly. He doesn't look up from the files.

"Well, that's great," I mutter and realize my hands are shaking.

"I'm not sure how you pulled it off, but these death certificates from the coroner are pretty enlightening," he says and finally lays them down.

"Hey, I'm in remission and I have places to go, so I'll see you later Wilson."

"I want to know how you gave it back to them, how you reversed all you did to heal them. If your grandfather had the ability as healer to do that, I never heard of him doing it."

Sweat breaks out across my brow and my heart races.

"I was dying! What was I supposed to do?" I scream at him.

"You have something I can't explain. I knew your grandfather and he never, ever would have done this to the very people he tried to help!"

"I'm not my grandfather! He could expel the disease from his body! I can't do that. It stayed and rotted me from the insides. It was killing me to help them," I exclaim. My blood is boiling and I can feel my face grow hot in anger. Guilt fills me and I hate what I've done, but I couldn't do anything.

"So you killed them?"

"No, I made everything right again. I gave them the instrument of their death back. I put everything right again."

He looks at me and hangs his head low. Slowly, he closes the file and glances back up at me. Inside, I still want to smash my fists into his face, to make him feel some sort of pain. Maybe then he'd be more sympathetic.

"You stole the gift of life they were given. You stole their second chance," he says and walks around the desk.

"What about my life? What about this fucking curse of mine? Maybe I wanted to live and have a second chance. I wanted my chance back."

"No second chances," he whispers in my ear and I feel something slide into my side, just under my ribs.

"Wilson?" I utter. I back away from him and see the blood drip from the scalpel in his outstretched hand. My second chance blooms on my white tee shirt and forms a puddle on the floor.

"You killed them. You're a monster."

Dropping to my knees, I look up at him and black creeps in around the corners of my vision.

"I didn't want to die," I mutter to him and fall to the soft brown carpet floor.

I can hear him sob. Maybe he realizes he's no better than me now.

No second chance for me either.

So cold.

Fuck.

***

STORY NOTES:

This is another one written specially for a submission call with a theme. The call wanted a story where the author dies in the end. We got to write our own deaths. For those who don't know me, the Brent in the story is a way bigger asshole than I am, but I think some of his feelings toward dying are shared by both of us. It took me a few tries to get the story to line out in my head. Once I realized the best way for me to extend my life was to take back the life I'd given others, it flowed very easily from my head to the keyboard. The doctor who killed me might have a tough go in the fiction world later… I mean he did kill me.

THE MIDNIGHT FAIR

Long ago in the town of Thorney, a town forgotten by time, the first cool winds of fall began to blow through the rundown village. Racing against the oncoming frost, the farmers harvested their meager crops from another harsh summer. The men spent their days picking what remained of the corn and thrashing the sagging wheat. What little food they managed to scavenge from the fields had to be preserved and the breads baked in preparation for the cold, brutal winter that would soon be upon them. Even the children worked in the fields with their fathers, bringing home baskets to their mothers, and then returning with water for the weary men still toiling. One of these boys was Arthur, who tended to laze about or one would find his head floating in clouds of fancy. Dusk was quickly approaching one October evening when Arthur first saw the hand bills for the fair blowing down the cobbled streets of Thorney.

Earlier in the evening Arthur's mother grew tired of him being under her foot while she tried to cook dinner for her husband and Arthur's older brothers. Working in the fields was harsh for the men, but the harvest had to be completed in three weeks because Thorney's first frost came on All Saints Day every year like clockwork. When his mother swatted at him with the broom to get him out of the way, Arthur ran out of the cottage and gave a quick wave to his father and brothers in the field as he headed towards town to watch the sun set.

Dusk started to settle when Arthur stepped on the Thorney Bridge. He gazed out and admired the cloud's colors in the fading sunlight. Leaning over, he gasped in amazement at how beautiful the reflection in the river was. The water stood still and the reflection reminded Arthur of a mirror, where the sky stopped and the water began was difficult for him to tell. He backed away from the bridge's railing and noticed how quiet it had become. He glanced back and forth to each side of the bridge, but he could not hear or see anyone. The sun's descent was almost completed and the rundown roof line of the town shrouded the cobblestone streets in shadows. The wind began to pick up and Arthur suddenly felt cold, as if an ice cube had been dropped down his shirt.

In the distance from the outskirts of town, came a rumbling. Torch lights illuminated the streets as the roaring thunder of hooves approached Arthur. He dove to the side of the bridge when the horse drawn carriages and wagons sped past him. All the horses were black as coal and to Arthur they snorted hellfire when they looked his way. Twelve wagons and carriages passed him by and disappeared far off on the other side of town. He stood up and brushed himself off wondering what all the commotion was about. The evening air grew chilly as a breeze returned from the west. He heard a fluttering on the opposite end of the bridge, like a deck of cards being released into the air. A paper floated over to him and dropped at his feet. He bent over and picked up the yellowed, aged parchment and read it.

"Come One, Come All! Enter the Fair of the Macabre! For One Night and Day Only! Have Your Every Wish Become Reality! See Our Collection of Lost Souls! Enter At Your Own Risk!"

A fair! Arthur grew very excited about what he would find there. He felt in his pocket and a couple of coins greeted his fingers. Rolling the gold pieces between his fingertips, he smiled and headed off towards the other side of town.

***

Throughout Thorney, as the full moon rose in the sky, and the wind began to howl, handbills for the fair blew onto every doorstep in town. They fluttered on windowsills and door mats, making an awful racket in the quiet night. The windows that sat darkened moments before began to glow with candlelight while the town folk read the fliers they were picking up off of the ground. Arthur's father was already up, waiting for their son to return home. His father looked outside once more and the paper fell upon his feet for him to read. Scanning it over, he knew Arthur must be there. He woke his wife and told her he knew where Arthur was at and was leaving to fetch him. She mumbled under her veil of sleep about milking the cows while he was out and nodded off once more.

Opening the door into the night, Arthur's father found many of his friends and fellow farmers stepping out and watched the others coming out of their homes. The men were the only ones who came outside and each held the handbill in their grasp. All thirty of them glanced around at each other and nodding, started to walk towards the ramshackle buildings that constituted the downtown area. They formed a single file line and trudged off towards the fair to answer the calling they heard echoing through their heads. The line moved in silence.

Arthur saw the men coming towards him and dove behind a stone pillar. He knew if his father caught him out, he would be in for a beating. He watched in silence as his father led the line past his hiding spot. They hung their heads down and marched like in a funeral procession. He shifted to the right a bit and a pebble under his foot rolled down the embankment into the river with a splash. His father turned to the sound and scanned the area. Arthur ducked down and held his breath so that he didn't make the slightest sound. Shaking his head, his father motioned for the men to carry on.

When the group disappeared on the other side of the bridge, Arthur crawled out from his haven and followed the men. He found the bridge harder to navigate as the moon went behind a cloud. Without the beams illuminating the cobblestones, Arthur slowed up and held onto the bridge's side so he wouldn't fall. One step at a time, he cautiously moved after the faint orange glow from the men's torches. Closing in on the bridge's end, he heard a grunt and cough in front of him. Squinting, he examined the creeping darkness. The blackness coughed again, closer this time. Arthur felt his insides clench up, anxiously waiting for the cough's source to reveal itself.

A hand fell on his shoulder and Arthur screamed.

"Nothing good that way boy," muttered the gravelly voice before breaking into another cough. The person struck a match and lit the pipe clenched in his mouth.

"Mister Rusticap, what brings you out here?"

"Promises to keep and prices to pay my boy, and we all must pay the price eventually."

"Were you with my father and the other men?"

He chuckled and grabbed Arthur on the shoulders and shaking him said, "Turn back now. Those men have a date at the Midnight Fair and it's not a place for young men."

"But I have to follow my father Mister Rusticap. I'm curious about a fair that the farmers go to in the night. I like fairs."

Rusticap turned around till his back was towards Arthur. Arthur heard him hiss in pain when he pulled his shirt up over his shoulders. The moonbeams returned and lit up Rusticap's back. A pentagram spanned his back from his neck to the base of his spine. Fluid oozed down from the shape and remained slick from the fresh blood. Arthur moved up for a closer look. He gasped when he saw the pins and needles that pierced his flesh and each point formed the outline of the symbol. Rusticap rotated his shoulder blades and new blood flowed down from the wounds. Wincing some more, he pulled his shirt back down and rolled his shoulders around so his shirt settled on his back in more comfortable manner.

"What happened to your back Mister Rusticap? What's the star for?"

"I paid my price and those men are going to do the same for the bargain they will make. The star is a symbol for the banker who cashed in my loan and gave me what I needed. Arthur, be careful, for all things have a price and payment is not always what it seems to be. Ah, I blather on like the old man I am and the hour grows late. Go on now; I suggest you return to your mother and brothers, because nothing good comes out of the fair for someone your age."

He inhaled deeply of the sweet smelling tobacco and made little circles that drifted into the night and vanished. He reached down and patted Arthur on the head and turned him back towards home. Rusticap turned and wandered aimlessly back into the shadows of the buildings. The footsteps faded into silence and Arthur turned around and finished crossing the bridge. The fair awaited him.

***

The trees covered the roadway and clenched down around him like a fist. Arthur felt the eyes and things in the woods watch him. He scanned the tree line and saw the small specs of light reflecting the moonlight on the woodland creature's eyes. His breath quickened and his pace increased into a run. The clearing called to him, to give him sanctuary from the ominous night, and to lead him to his father. The running did have an unintended consequence however; it allowed him to gain ground on the men even though his conversation with Rusticap put him behind.

The conversation left him with many questions about price and how you pay it. Mister Rusticap left him confused as to the whole transaction thing. When his father needed something, he got some coins from the (supposedly hidden) place the coins were kept and paid for the good or service then. He remembered in hard times, his father paid either in crops or labor. In his whole eleven years of existence, he never remembered a time when his father paid for something by having pins jabbed into his back in a star design. Arthur shuddered, remembering the hamburger like texture in places on Mister Rusticap's raw and bleeding back.

Lost in his thought, Arthur ran into a sign and fell backwards onto the dry, drought hardened ground. Wincing in pain, he looked up and saw the sign for "Mr. Natas's Circus of the Damned and Macabre Midnight Fair". Below the banner, a poster rippled on the fence post showing a man in a big red top hat and a bright red suit. His eyes looked like they were ablaze and his maniacal smile showcased his shinning white teeth. Below him, he stood on twelve dwarves and a man with scales around his face. Each one held the ringmaster aloft and each one grimaced in immense anguish and pain, but each entity gazed up at their master in reverence. The poster sent a shiver down Arthur's spine. Rubbing his arms to dispel of the goosebumps, he crawled under the fence railing and found himself surrounded by the fair's tents and booths.

Arthur peeked around the corner and found that all the canvas tents were faded, torn, and dilapidated. The once bright reds and oranges were bleached from years touring in the sun, each tattered edge wavering in the breeze. The booth he was crouched in front of left flakes of paint on his shirt as he brushed against it. The sign above it creaked, swaying back and forth. He craned his head up to read it.

"Wheel of Fortune, that is what my dad needs," he muttered, getting back to his feet.

He reached down and wiped the paint flecks from his clothes and slowly maneuvered through the maze of guide wires and tent stakes. Arthur stuck his tiptoe out into the darkness to feel his way around. Tripping was a very good way to get caught snooping around a fair after dark he supposed. Rounding a tent that boasted it contained the "Pin Man"; his path became illuminated by torches posted around the biggest tent Arthur had ever seen. Rising to a full stand, he bumped his head on the Pin Man sign. He rubbed the spot where the sign connected with his forehead and turned to get a good look at it. The man being advertised on the poster was Mister Rusticap.

The poster was different from the other older ones he had seen, this one seemed new. He stuck his nose up close to it and when he inhaled, he could smell the brightly colored inks still drying. The picture shook him to his core and he turned away quickly. In the image, Rusticap was suspended from the top of the big tent by the pins and needles in his back. Blood dripped from his side into the audience and they were illustrated laughing and wiping the gore on their arms and faces. Rusticap's own face gazed out dead and blank, his expression sullen and beaten. Arthur dropped back to his knees and swiftly crawled away from the disturbing poster.

A knot tightened in his stomach and it drew tighter with every inch he covered on the ground. The words Rusticap told him rattled around in his skull and he started to think he made a mistake following his father. He stopped and tried to gather up the nerve to either continue or turn tail and run back to his mother. Taking a few deep breaths, he closed his eyes and stood back up.

"I'm eleven and I'm not a baby," he whispered into the silent night. When it came out, it sounded like a plea with himself to carry on.

He took one last breath and exhaled with a whistle. The big tent awaited, his father and the other farmers were inside. He greatly wanted to see what the men were up to so he could tell his friends tomorrow. Arthur hoped the men were making a deal for all the kids to spend the day at the fair. If he came home with that kind of information, he thought they would hail him as a king! He continued on and found himself at the edge of the big tent. Arthur rolled underneath the ratty canvas and crouching behind a crate next to him, listened to the men.

***

"Gentlemen, you know the deal. Your time has expired and I am here to either collect or make another arrangement," said the man in the middle with the big red top hat.

The other men sat in the stands in a small cluster. All of them stared at the ground; none of them looked directly at the man pacing back and forth like a caged tiger before them. He stopped and while looking into the crowd, picked his teeth. The ringmaster looked at the maggot he pulled out from between his teeth and flicked it on the ground. It landed with a hiss and caught fire, burning until it was nothing more than ash.

"I'm really growing tired of your hesitation. A generation ago, your fathers sat right where you sit now mulling the same choice. Do you really know how deep this reaches? For five generations your families have waited for me to bring my fair into town. Some make, shall we say, personal arrangements while the farmers band together and ask for what you want to ask me for. How dry was the summer? How are your crops this harvest with the frost quickly approaching?" The man smiled and turned back to the crate where Arthur hid. Arthur knew the man saw him because their gazes locked and the ringmaster's eyes suddenly blazed up a bright orange. He gently placed his finger to his lips, signaling Arthur to remain silent and turned back to the men.

A man stood up and Arthur saw it was his father.

"What would you have us do? I know the town has paid for our crops; my father alluded to that on his deathbed. I ask you, what is this price?" Arthur's father asked before sitting back down.

"Funny you should ask. Five families have paid me in the past and the circle closes as those who have not paid will be asked to do so. You even brought with you the preferred method of payment."

There was a rustle behind Arthur and he turned his head slowly around to see what the noise behind him was. Rusticap stood there, his dead eyes staring back at him. He shook his head in disgust at Arthur and shambled out into the center of the tent. He stopped before the ringmaster and hung his head low.

"Now, now, now Rusticap is that anyway to appear in my presence?"

"No, Dr. Natas. Please forgive me," he pleaded weakly, his voice a mere whisper.

A loud clanking echoed throughout the tent as chains shot down from the shadows in the top of the tent, knocking Rusticap down to the ground. He landed on his stomach and they quickly went to work hooking themselves into the pins and needles in his back. Once they were attached they yanked him from the floor and swung his body out over the farmers. They stared in shock at Rusticap's fate. His blood dripped down on them like a spring rain while he continued to ascend into the darkness above.

"You see what happens to those who don't follow my rules. Now then, Richard, last time your father lost the straw pull. He made a deal to take someone else instead of you. He couldn't bear the thought of losing his only son. Your life is because of me. Your son was the price your father paid for you. You are blessed; you have three other sons who will in turn give you many grandsons. What is the loss of one for the life of a town? Surrender your son to me or the crops will continue to wither and die along with the town. The frost is only days away and I can give you what you need to survive the winter."

The men one by one turned their heads to look at Richard. Arthur stood up from behind the crate and ran through the ring to his father. His legs moved as fast as they could carry them and his tears flowed from his eyes. His father jumped down from the benches and ran to his son, his arms open. They met in the middle and embraced, both weeping.

Dr. Natas began clapping slowly. He wiped his eyes with his sleeve and began laughing. "So touching, really. Now it's time gentlemen. The boy or the town? The boy or your own kin? What say you?"

The men started to clamor at Richard to give Arthur to Natas. Their yelling grew louder and each shout became more aggressive. Richard squeezed his son harder and his tears ran down Arthur's back.

"I love you son. I will always love you no matter what happens."

"D… dad? I'm scared," Arthur managed to say between his crying.

"We all must pay the price," his father whispered in his ear as he gave his son one last squeeze and let him go.

"NO! Father, NO!" Arthur bellowed, reaching out towards his father. Richard looked away and closed his eyes, fighting with everything he had to not rush back to his son.

The rattling sounded out as Rusticap descended from the ceiling and grabbed Arthur on the shoulders, his fingers digging into his flesh. Arthur gave one last whimpering plea for his father to help him before he was violently jerked upwards into the blackness above their heads. Richard fell to his knees in the center ring.

Natas came over and placed his hand on Richard's head. Leaning over he whispered in his ear, "The most painful thing is to lose a son. My father exiled me, but I think he only cared more about his image than anything else. I want you to turn around and look at the faces of these men. You have saved the town for a generation, your price is paid and your town shall flourish once again."

Natas stood up and looked back at the men, "your duty has been performed, go now and let your children come back and frolic through the fair in the morning before we pull stakes and move on. Oh wait, there is one last thing," he paused as a chain dropped down and carried a chalice down to him, "this must be sprinkled around the farms to feed the crops. You will have food for the winter."

Natas handed the chalice to Richard and faded into the shadows. The fluid that filled the chalice was red. Richard leaned back and searched the darkness above, as his son screamed out his name over and over again. The other men came down from the benches and helped him to his feet. One tried to take the chalice away, afraid Richard might drop it before they returned to their farms. Richard clutched it tighter to his chest and the others decided to let him carry it home as his own burden, their own consciences now clear.

The trip back was in silence. When they returned a few hours before dawn, they sprinkled Arthur's blood on the fields. It only took a small splash on each field. Field by field, they marched on performing the rite until all their fields had been sanctified. The men departed without a word and returned to their homes and sleeping families, none of which would ever speak the truth of the past night.

Richard stumbled back to his field and held the chalice to his chest. Looking down, he realized the last remnants of his son rested in the bottom of the golden cup. In the moonlight he used the last of Arthur on the field. Fulfilling his duty, he tried to think about his son, but for some reason the memories became cloudy and he found it harder to remember him. Gathering his thoughts, he went to work doing his last bit of work for the night.

As the town of Thorney awoke the next morning, the fields miraculously turned green overnight with crops ready to be harvested for the winter.

One man came to thank Richard for something he couldn't quite remember and found him in the field, hanging from the elm tree at the back of his farm. His body swayed in the early morning breeze and the coldness of death kept the chalice gripped tightly in his hands.

Later in the day, the children frolicked at the fair and nobody remembered an Arthur.

***

STORY NOTES:

This story was originally published by the name, "As I Went Over Lincoln Bridge". The anthology called for expanding on nursery rhymes in rather dark ways. I found a little known rhyme that served as the title for the story. In it, I really begin my fixation on sacrifice and loss. There are bits of these themes running in most everything I do and comes out in my White Creek novel and the stories set in the town. The main point of the story turns from Arthur following the men to the fair to when you have to choose between one person and a whole village, how does one handle that choice? What are the ramifications of that choice? The story became darker than what I intended, but it fits it in the long run.

WINDS OF WAR

May 6th, 1915 - Midnight

The full moon shimmered on the Atlantic's black waves as they crashed against the ship's hull. Felix took another long pull from his whiskey flask and sighed heavily. He loved the ocean at night and always joined a crew whenever he could, but he missed his wife and daughter. Chuckling, he remembered how his mother scolded and admonished him for being like his father, who also felt the call of the sea, but the doctor bills for his beloved little girl Helen kept him at the water's mercy.

She'd always been jealous 'cause the sea was dad's mistress and she was only a port of call, he thought to himself.

The salty ocean breeze picked up around him and he pulled his coat tighter around him. The May air chilled him more than it usually did and the events from the docks in New York a few days before left the crew unsettled and the unaccounted for sailors didn't help calm the fears running rampant through the ship. Before setting sail, the passengers, crew, and cargo from the commandeered vessel *Cameronia* became the *Lusitania's* problem to deal with. The whole crew and Captain Turner thought it a bad omen to set out to sea under such strange auspices, but the *Lusitania* was due in Europe and the rich on the cruise ship had no patience.

Then there were the disappearances.

A hollow tapping broke the night's still silence. Felix lifted his head and glanced around. His eyes swept the deck and he didn't notice anything out of the ordinary. Trying in vain, he couldn't shake the feeling someone was watching him.

Feeling uneasy, Felix craned his head around, but the starboard walkway remained still and quiet. The swaying lamps in the breeze threw shadows all about the walls and railings. Wisps of fog curled around the railing and settled on the walkway. Snorting, he tossed back another shot of the 'old rot gut' and fell to the deck.

Cursing, he felt the back of his head and felt the fresh flowing blood. Head spinning, he tried to get up when something crashed on the deck beyond the foggy veil.

"What the…" he muttered before the lamps blinked out, leaving him in only the moon's eerie glow.

Felix swung his head from side to side trying to home in on the rustling closing in all around him. Getting to his knees, he violently jerked upwards and slammed into the metal deck stairs. He cried out and a cold hand covered his mouth from behind, silencing him. Felix closed his eyes and tried to scream. At first the pain in his neck reminded him of a small pin prick, but it soon erupted into a massive throbbing. The ripping and tearing became sucking sounds and Felix felt paralyzed. Sensing his life-blood drain away on his coat and on the stranger's smacking lips, he thanked God when the twinge in his throat ceased and he flew over the railing, splashing down into the murky sea sinking down in the depths in eternal slumber.

***

"Man overboard! Man overboard! Quickly, to the starboard side!" cried the watchman from the crow's nest.

Three sailors ran to the railing and peered down, searching the murky black ocean surface. A flare lit up the dark and one flew over the side and illuminated the water. None of the men saw nor heard any splash or shouting from below. Another grabbed the life preserver from the deck wall and tossed it out, hoping to save whoever tumbled from the side. The men shouted to one another, trying to get a plan of action.

"We need to inform the Captain," ordered one of the men.

"Sir, what do we tell him? Do we have him turn back to look? Let's just forget we were out here and go back inside, the fog's rolling in and it looks thick," answered the older, stockier figure.

A metallic flip echoed on the walkway and they turned to see a man light a cigarette. He took a deep, long drag from it and flicked it over the rail. The men watched the glowing ember float to the ocean surface and extinguish in the waves.

"Going back to your cabins is a pretty good idea gents," the man said with a gruff voice. The man stepped out of the shadows and stood before them in a tan trench coat and a brown fedora pulled down over his face, shrouding it in darkness.

"Who're you?"

"I'm about to save your life. Go back to your cabins, lock the door, and don't come out again until sun up."

"What's this about? You ain't no part of the crew, so why should we listen to you?"

"Take me to your captain and I will explain everything to him," the stranger said, digging another smoke out of his pocket.

"Ok, come with me and I'll take you to Captain Turner," the biggest of the crewmen offered and motioned for the man to follow him.

After a short jaunt down the outside walkway, they arrived at the captain's quarters. The crewman pounded his fist on the door and waited.

A rough and tired voice called out, "Who's there?"

"Jenson sir, and I have a guest who demands to see you."

"Gimmie a moment," Captain Turner said and they heard shuffling and couching from inside the cabin. After a few minutes, the door opened and he poked his head out. "What's this all about now, it's after midnight?"

The man in the trench coat spoke up, "I needed to see you Captain Turner. It's a matter of life and death."

"Very well, come in. Jenson, you are excused."

Jenson turned and left leaving the captain and the man.

"Come in; please come in, mister...?"

"Hammers."

"Well Mr. Hammers, please let us have a drink and you can tell me what this is all about," Turner said while he turned and retreated into his cabin.

Hammers began when the door shut, "Captain Turner,"

"Bill, please call me Bill," he said pouring two glasses of brandy.

"Four days ago, you were detained at port in New York City. Do you know why?"

"I was ordered to take on forty-one passengers, crew, and cargo from the *Carmonia*," he answered passing the glass to Hammers.

"Did they have any bulky cargo? Was there something strange on their manifest perhaps? I'm looking for three crates that three German fellows are in possession of. I believe those men were part of the forty-one you inherited in port. When I found your sailors on the deck, they were discussing covering up a man going overboard."

"Another man overboard? That is the fourth one since we set out and that doesn't count the others we can't find. The German men? They're not listed on the manifest and our initial head count was accurate, everyone at the dock is listed and accounted for. Are you sure about these men?" Turner asked.

"So the rumors are true," Hammers muttered to himself and looked up to Captain Turner, "look, we need to find those German men and detain them. If we don't find them I believe more than just the sailors or a few missing passengers will perish."

"Who are you?" Turner inquired. The stranger made him uncomfortable and he meant to get to the bottom of why he felt that way.

"I'm with military intelligence. Whatever those men brought on this ship is bound to Europe where couriers will deliver the crates to the Kaiser. We believe those crates can tip the balance of the war effort in Europe," Hammers explained and removing his ID from his coat pocket slid it across the table to Captain Turner.

Turner picked up the badge and studied it for a moment. "What do you suggest?"

"First we need to make sure everyone, including the crew, remains in their cabin tonight. In the morning at breakfast, we will do a search to find the Germans and whatever it is they brought aboard the boat. I hope we aren't too late."

"Too late?"

"Yes, too late. If whatever they have gets loose, it might already be beyond our control."

"How will you get back to your cabin Mr. Hammers?"

"I'll be fine; I have experience in these matters."

"Will you not tell me what I'm dealing with on my ship?"

"No, because then I'd have to kill you," he answered with a wink and got up from the table.

Opening the door, Turner turned, "will I die anyway?'

"I hope not, but you never know," Hammers smirked walking out into the night.

Turner looked around the deck outside his cabin door and shuddered. He'd spent a lot of time on the open sea and he had a very bad feeling about the trip. The atmosphere seemed darker than before he opened his door. Turner closed it again and crawled into bed, hoping morning's light would bring a better day.

May 6th, 1915 - Morning

Hammers already sat outside the dining hall doors when Captain Turner, Jenson, and two other men arrived.

"Morning gentlemen, I believe you have the passenger manifest?" Hammers asked rolling an unlit smoke around his fingers.

Turner handed him the binder and shook his head. "Don't know what you want with those. Everyone listed was counted and cleared before we set sail."

Hammers flipped through the pages, examining every name and committing them to memory. Grimacing he reached out to hand the binder back.

"What's wrong?" Turner questioned.

"The manifest for the *Cameronia* is incomplete. You told me forty-one passengers were moved here, but where is the paperwork for their baggage? Is there a way to get everyone back to their cabins and begin a room-by-room search? Somewhere there are three dangerous people we need to talk to or more will die."

"You heard the man, let's get the passengers back to their cabins. Jenson and Buttons you take the aft and me and Hammers will take the port," Turner ordered and handed part of the passenger manifest to Jenson.

"Meet back here at three o' clock sharp. Good luck," Hammers said as he and Turner went to make the announcement.

The passengers were unhappy hearing the flu bug ran rampant on the ship, but it was the best way Hammers could come up with. When people started to raise questions, they needed a plausible explanation for keeping them in their cabins.

May 6th, 1915 - 3:45 pm

"Hammers we're late," snorted Turner.

"Look, we have three more cabins left and we have to be sure everything is fine."

Hammers reached out and knocked on 3145's door. With a heavy thump, something slammed onto the floor inside. A low moan emanated from the other side.

"Hello? This is the captain and I need to inspect your cabin," Turner said sternly, the authority rolling off his tongue.

The movement ceased and the room grew silent again.

Hammers knocked one last time and drew his gun. Turner stared at the silver Colt in amazement.

"Permission to enter cabin sir?" Hammers quipped.

"Permission granted, let's see what the blazes is going on in there."

One swift kick jarred the flimsy wooden door from its hinges. It crashed to the floor and the men peered inside. The black room looked like an open mouth waiting to devour anything drawing near. From where they stood they saw the bed sheets covering the porthole, blocking any light from getting in the cabin. The room stank of human waste and sickness. Buzzing flies emerged from the black and flew off down the hallway.

The men covered their mouths and noses with their sleeves and headed into the room. Hammers flung the bathroom door open and pointed his Colt inside. Darkness welcomed him and he flicked his lighter on.

The orange glow threw shadows around the bathroom. The flickering flame showed nothing hiding or amiss in the tiny closet sized space. Cautiously backing out into the room, he stopped and listened.

"I don't hear anything. No movement, breathing, or anything," Hammers whispered.

Both stood still and held their breaths. The only sound came from the ocean waves striking the sides of the moving vessel.

"Under the bed, I heard something," Turner pointed to the small bed. The blankets were thrown about and lay strewn across the floor.

Hammers handed the lighter to Turner and slowly climbed down to his hands and knees. Leaning his neck further, he tilted his head and checked under the bed. Turner knelt and brought light to the shadows. Wadded covers blocked his view of the space under the bed. Hammers reached out and gently taking hold of a corner, pulled.

Turner handed the lighter to Hammers and he scanned beneath the bed finding nothing. Gently standing, he fell back down, the lamp connecting to his shoulder. Turner turned and saw a shape in the corner, veiled by the cover of darkness.

"Leave me now. You are trespassing in my room," a low, guttural voice ordered.

"Are you ok? There are reports of the flu amongst the crew and we are checking on everyone," Turner said.

"I'm not feeling well. Since last night after my walk, I've felt feverish. Please help an old woman to the doctor," the said lightening in tone.

Turner went to the hallway and called out to a passing steward, "Please come help us get a sick passenger to the doctor."

The steward rushed into the room and looked at the woman in the corner shadows.

She reached out pleading, "Help me please."

Knowing his duty is to the beck and call of the guests, he reached back to take her hands.

The scream pierced the close confined space in the cabin. The steward pulled his hand back and in the lighter's flame they saw the blood pouring from a gaping wound in the back of his hand. The old woman jumped on the bed and lunged for Hammers. He looked into her eyes and knew it was too late. Lightning quick, he brought the Colt to bear and pulled the trigger.

The deafening shot blew a hole in her chest and threw her body back into the wall like a rag doll. Turner and the steward flinched back from the thunderous echo and Hammers rushed to the woman.

Lying on the floor, she grabbed Hammers' pant leg and tugged him down. Her body rolled on top of him and her jaws snapped at his face. Her breath crept up his nose and the smell of decay made him gag. He felt the tips of her newly pointed teeth press into his coat. His fingers searched around, trying to find something to help get her off of him. The other two men stood frozen in fear and he knew he was on his own.

Feeling around closer to the wall, his fingers found the blanket covering the window and he yanked it free from the porthole. Sunlight poured in through the glass, illuminating the cabin. The rays fell on the floor and covered the woman in the bright light. Screaming in agony, she writhed around and jumped up to her feet.

Hammers watched her skin bubble and pulsate. White foam dripped from her maw and her ember hued eyes bulged in her skull. The room brightened and with a loud pop, her body exploded, showering the three men in gore.

"What the Hell was that Hammers?" Turner yelled wiping the crimson gunk from his arms and face.

"That my friends, was a vampire. The three German men? I can't believe I didn't figure it out sooner. I've waited since day one for them and they were right under my nose. The cargo is three stone sarcophaguses containing the last known vampires on Earth and they are the three supposed Germans I've been sent after. Damn, they're not Germans at all. The Kaiser wants them to tip the balance of the war so that Europe falls under Germany's yoke. If those creatures reach the Deutschland, the war is lost. They will create an army of those things."

"Why were they in America?" Turner asked, his face growing paler by the moment.

"After Cornwallis surrendered to Washington at Yorktown to end the Revolutionary War, all British ships in the harbor fell under our control. One of the ships was inbound with a set of fail-safes for Cornwallis should he find himself losing. The ship contained three creatures captured in Romania by a British explorer who gave them to King George in 1774. Once the war started swinging in the colonist's favor, he dispatched them to turn the tide. Thankfully, they never arrived in time."

"How'd the Germans get them?"

"We're not sure and it's a question I'd love to ask them."

"How are going to handle the situation on my ship? I have a crew and passengers to think about and protect."

"This," Hammer said and grabbed the steward by the throat, shoving him against the wall.

"What? That woman bit my hand!" the steward yelled.

"Stop. It. Now. First, what's your name?"

"Irving Smith and I've been with the crew for six years. Why?"

"Do you want to live?"

"Yes."

"Good, I'll need your help. If we don't destroy the three master vampires tonight, you'll become one by morning," Hammers said and let go of his throat.

Irving rubbed the bruised place on his neck where Hammers choked him. Something roiled within him, an anger and rage he'd never felt before. The burning sensation in his hand ceased and sweat already dripped down his forehead while the virus's hooks dug in. A knot formed in his stomach and he wanted to vomit. Deep down, the internal changes rapidly began and he embraced them. Voices called out in his head from the others who had fallen under the vampire's spell. He heard all who had been infected and knew they held the upper hand. Hammers would pay for treating him like a dog. He sensed his brethren gathering in the ship and decided to play along, biding his time.

May 6th, 1915 - 4:59 pm

"Ok men, we don't have much time left. I want an announcement made that all passengers and unessential crew are to board the life rafts tonight. The flu outbreak has reached a critical stage and we need to get them off the ship. While they are evacuating, we will begin sweeping the lower decks for the three vampires," explained Hammers. Tossing a bag to Captain Turner, he unrolled the ship's map.

"What is the plan?" asked Jensen as he took the wooden stake from Turner.

"Somewhere below deck, is their nest. The missing passengers and crew are sure to be changed by now. Irving here will be a vampire by morning if we don't kill the original three. Each original we slay, their progeny die because the link between them is severed."

"How do you know so much Mr. Hammers?" Irving inquired.

"My family has hunted them for hundreds of years and it is my mission to know about them, my life depends on it."

Jensen turned and saluted Hammers, "I'm with you and Captain Turner. Where do we begin?"

"Once we make the proper preparations, we head to only the biggest and darkest place on the ship... the cargo hold," Hammers said and walked out the door.

May 6th, 1915 - 8:20 pm

The sun fell below the horizon and the men finished gathering on the main deck. A quick run through the ship allowed them to shut the different sections of the ship off from each other. If the vampires needed to run, their choices of locations would be severely limited.

Ten men stayed in the radio and control room to keep the ship on course. The other eight grabbed lanterns and stakes, prayed, and descended down into the deep underbelly of the vessel.

"Ok men, this is it. The men up here in the wheel house are our last line of defense. If anything goes wrong, this location is our regrouping point," Hammers said and unrolled the ship schematics on the table. "We will proceed down the main stairwell in the center of the ship to the second deck. From there, we'll check the cargo hold and then the engine room. Any questions?"

Jensen spoke up first, "Yeah, when do we begin?"

"Right now," Hammers said and grabbing his lantern exited into the night.

The eight men followed, knowing they walked in the shadow of death. In the unusually chilly air, sweat dotted their brows and fear rattled in their bones.

Irving brought up the rear smiling without the sweat or the fear and a new hunger burning through his body.

***

The slow and steady trek to the cargo hold took four hours through the winding decks of the *Lusitania*. Double checking the ship took longer than they expected and the sun was gone long before they reached the bowls of the ship. Silence filled the hallways and the ship seemed empty, devoid of life. The only light emanated from the three lanterns spread out through the men. Reaching their destination, they stopped and stared at the metal doors guarding the unknown.

Hammers stretched out his hand and grabbed the latch. Slowly lifting it up, he heard the rusted mechanism groan as it disengaged. The men huddled closer and Hammers gently pushed the heavy door open.

The hinges cried out and scurrying rats ran for cover under the boxes and steamer trunks. The nauseating air hit their nostrils and a few doubled over heaving from the stench. Hammers stepped in and swept the area inside the door with the lantern's light. Something hit his foot and he looked down. A rat holding a finger rushed by and exited the hold. Blood pooled near his foot where the rat sat seconds before. Following the red trail and the buzzing flies, the light settled on a festering pile of bodies. Ripped pieces of flesh hung from the exposed bones and teeth marks pocked the necks and arms.

"I thought there'd be more blood," Turner stated covering his mouth and nose with his sleeve.

"This is their feeding pit. Most of the missing would have been brought here to nourish the fledgling vampires," Hammers whispered partly in shock by the sheer number of dead bodies before him.

"What do we do now?" Turner asked.

"We get the engine room as soon as possible. Night has fallen and we need to end this now," Hammers said turning toward the door.

Jensen and the cook next to him screamed in surprise and horror. Irving buried himself in Jensen's neck. His jaws clamped down, chewing deep into the arteries, spraying his face in a bloody shower. His clawed fingers dug into the cook's neck, tearing into his throat and splashing the crimson fluid on Hammers and Turner.

Turner spun around, throwing himself out of the hold. Hammers drew his Colt and fired at the feeding vampire. The shot caught him in the shoulder and he flew off Jensen, slamming into the cold steel wall.

Irving stood up, brushing his shoulders off.

"That tickles," he said mocking Hammers.

"Yeah, but this won't," Hammers retorted and rushed toward the new vampire.

Both locked up and the stake in Hammers hand fell to the floor. Irving swiped his claws across Hammers' chest and blood welled up through his shirt on the deep gashes.

Hammers ran his fingers over the wounds and stared at the red staining his fingertips wincing.

"Oh, I've waited for this all day," Irving said, his tongue rolling across his fangs.

"I bet you have," Turner said ramming the stake through Irving's back. The tip broke through and pierced his heart.

Irving shook and howled in agony. The hole in his back flamed up and the fire immolated his body in a blinding flash. His face melted like wax and his remains pooled on the floor. The flames burnt out and died away leaving a black pool of fluids and ash.

Behind Hammers and Turner in the hallway, the last three members of their team shouted. Down the long, dark hallway to the engine room, glints of red appeared. The fiery orbs multiplied and drew nearer. One of the crew threw their lantern at the oncoming horde. The kerosene ignited engulfing the hall in flames. Shrill cries echoed down the corridor and the men took advantage and ran to the stairs.

Sizzling flesh crackled and hair burned off the young vampires, their new powers too weak to survive the purifying flames. Behind the rabid pack of new converts were the three. Their forms shifted to huge gray wolves and barking loudly, they ran to the stairs in pursuit.

Hammers heard the creatures hurtle their bodies into the door until the wood gave out and exploded inward. Through the splintered shards, they dashed up the stairs. A portly fellow who worked in the washroom slipped on the carpeted stairs and fell. Rolling down a floor, the wolves pounced and tore into his body. The bloody foamy muzzles peeled the flesh from his bones and clawed into his stomach. Making one last ditch effort, he gripped the stake in his hand and drove it upward.

The wolf yelped and flipped around on its back. Swiftly, the wolf shifted back to a man, the stake sticking out of his chest. Closing his eyes and tilting his head back, his body caught fire. Burning hot and fast, his ashes exploded in the small stairwell.

Hammers looked down the staircase and flinched back. A column of ash shot up the stairs and dusted the men. The other two wolves stopped and howled. Hammers stopped and motioned for the others to freeze.

"They must have felt something when he died," Hammers said, mulling the turn of events.

"Was that one of the three?" Turner asked.

"I think so. They can shape shift," Hammers said, more to himself then to the others.

"What about them?"

"I need to get to the bridge immediately. We got lucky killing one, but I don't think we can take two more," Hammers mused. He ran his fingers over the deepening scarlet on his shirt. Wincing, he motioned for the others to move on while the vampires bayed to the night in shock.

May 7th, 1915 - 1:26 am

The waves crashed into the ship and the swaying made the last three hunters stumble from side to side trying to keep their balance. Wind swept through the outer deck areas and with most of the lights off, the vessel looked like a ghost ship floating in the abysmal Atlantic night. The passengers out on the sea stared in wonderment at the hundreds of shapes rushing around in the dimly lit ship.

The three shapes ran. Panting and cramping, they pushed on. A strange green mist flowed out the door onto the deck after them. Ahead, a door flew open and waves of the undead flowed onto the deck. Hammers grabbed Turner and hopped up a railing, avoiding the throbbing mass of vampires heading toward them. The crewman carrying up the rear fell and a mass of vampires descended down on him. His screams were cut short when his vocal cords were ripped out in a hungry creature's mouth.

Flailing arms reached and grabbed on to Turners pant legs, pulling him back down to the hungry undead horde. Kicking wildly, he connected to some of their heads and they backed off. Sharp finger nails tore through his pants and gouged his legs. Turner felt the streams of blood begin flowing from the wounds. Below, the vampires lapped at the drops raining down on them.

Hammers pulled again and Turner tumbled over the railing. Crashing to the deck, they looked at each other and nodded. Turning back, the mist floated up and the two remaining original vampires strolled out into the night air as the green faded away behind them. They ran toward the two men.

"We've lost her," Turner said shaking his head and running.

Hands gripped the railings and undead bodies flopped over the side onto the deck. Hammers and Turner kicked a few as they passed and ran to the bridge. The men inside saw them approach and opened the cumbersome metal door.

Pounding steps from hundreds of lost souls drew closer. Putting all their backs into it, they flung the bridge door closed and engaged the hefty lock bars.

Bodies thudded against the door, but it held. Turner looked around at the windows.

"Quickly, the windows!" Turner shouted.

The men jumped up and flung the tables and chairs over. Hurrying, the braced the furniture against the windows and sat against them to keep them in place. After a few minutes, the assault ceased and the deck outside grew silent.

"What happened?" Turner asked shooting a glance toward Hammers.

"I don't know. Is there a way of the bridge without going outside again?"

"Yes, we have a staircase that leads to a couple of lifeboats for the crew."

"Good, get everyone ready to head there," Hammers said and rushed to the controls.

Hammers grabbed the radio and found the secret broadcast station for the Navy.

"This is Alexander Hammers, authorization Alpha-Zulu-Foxtrot-Hotel. I am aboard the *Lusitania* and requesting Operation: Sunburst."

"This is Commander Vince Rice, authorization Tango-Whiskey-Beta-Zulu. Copy on Sunburst. We've shadowed the *Lusitania* for the last two days and are ready to go," the voice crackled over the receiver.

"The surviving passengers and crew have already abandoned ship and await your rescue. I also have the package."

"Copy that, boats are in the area to accept the passengers. On your mark, Sunburst is a go."

Turner turned to Hammers in shock, "You're sinking the *Lusitania?*"

"Yes, by this afternoon, this ship will be on the bottom of the Atlantic. Once the sun begins to rise, I want to sound the evacuation horns again once we begin to clear ourselves from the ship."

"What of the vampires?"

"The salt water will kill them. If they try to escape, the sun will kill them. Either way, they don't get into German hands," he said and patted his pant pocket.

Hammers got up and walked away from the captain and his remaining men. President Wilson wanted to get into the war and scrapping the *Lusitania* and blaming it on the German u-boats killed two birds with one stone. It ended the vampire threat and entered the US into World War I. Hammers shut his eyes for a moment and his thoughts became haunted by those who've died and by those who wish they would die.

"Get to the boats now," Hammers ordered the remaining men and they exited out the back hatch to the boats below.

May 7th, 1915 - 2:10 pm

The submarine dispatched by the US Navy sat off the rescue ship's stern. Hammers and Turner stood on the deck watching the other two boats leave with the survivors.

"What will happen now?" Turner asked.

"You're going to take the fall for this. Radio transmissions have already been recorded and the sub out there is sailing under a German designation."

"Why me? How can I face my countrymen when I return to London?"

"Deep down, know that everyone who speaks ill of you is alive because of you," Hammers said and patted Turner on the shoulder.

"Sir, we must go now," a Naval officer on the boat below the deck called up.

Turner and Hammers exchanged handshakes and climbed down the rope to the waiting dingy. Watching the *RMS Lusitania* they heard the torpedoes dart through the water, striking the haul. The explosion rocked the ocean and Turner kept his gaze on his beloved ship. He silently thanked the Lord it only took eighteen minutes to go under. He already knew when he returns home and his dreams haunted by it; he'll never get the dying sounds the vampires out of head for as long as he lives.

May 28th, 1915 - Germany: West of Beelitz

The military carrier reached into his bag and looked at the package. The plain brown wrapped box was to be seen by the Kaiser only. Having just been released from the hospital in

Beelitz, he was handed the assignment as a way to get him integrated back into the military.

A note scribbled on the side caught his attention. Instead of being in German, the note was in English and from America. Glancing around and seeing nobody watching, he ripped the wrapping off and tore into the box. Reaching in, he pulled out the contents and held it to the light. To him it looked like blood. Reading the message inside, Adolph Hitler folded it back up and placed it in his pocket next to the vial of vampire blood. A smile crossed his face and his mind began to contemplate his lucky find and what he could do with it.

***

STORY NOTES:

Vampires were never something I wanted to write about, but when a submission call opened up for alternate history horror, the idea popped into my head very quickly. Since I hold a degree in history, there were some puzzling events I had questions about. I focused on the Lusitania immediately. I always thought the US reason for getting involved in World War 1 seemed weak and I wanted to create a secret reason that forced our involvement or face an even bigger threat. What more could set it off than a luxury liner full of vampires bound for service in the German army? The very end came to me about halfway through writing the manuscript. I wanted to leave it open ended just in case I wanted to do something else with it later and Hitler's obsession with the occult was a natural place to leave it.

THE HEART'S LONGING

"Final boarding call for the 8:30 from White Creek to Chicago," the voice boomed over the intercom.

Cara White leaned in and kissed her boyfriend Jordan Grimm on the lips and smiled into his frown.

"Don't be such a downer, I'm only going to be a short train ride away," she said and flashed her smile at him. Two years ago, the same smile stole his heart and started them out on the journey they'd shared since then. He hated the idea that same smile wouldn't be around to see every day.

"I know, but you leaving for college and me being stuck here, really sucks," he answered, his voice trying to hide hurt inside.

She looked him over and shook her head.

"Thanks for wearing the classy Slayer shirt to say goodbye to me in."

"Oh, sorry," he muttered and glanced down at the pentagram on his faded black shirt.

The porter came by and loaded up the three suitcases Cara brought with her.

"Time to break it up folks, we have a schedule to keep," he quipped and quickly took her bags to the baggage car.

"I guess this is it," Jordan said and leaned in close. She answered by meeting his lips again in a long passionate kiss. Their tongues danced with each other and they drank deeply of their final moment together for the foreseeable future.

"I love you, Jordan Grimm," she said with a little laugh and a tear.

"I'll miss you, Cara," he answered back and let go of her hands, his fingertips lingering on hers before breaking contact.

Finally, with the engine starting to make noise, she climbed aboard and blew him one last goodbye. He reached out, snatched the kiss from the air and pretended to stick it in his pocket. She grinned again and waved as he mouthed the words, "I love you too". Jordan stuck his hands deep in his pockets and tried to force back the tidal waves of emotions rushing through him while the train departed.

The whistle cried out its long lonely wail and the chugging engine began pulling the 8:30pm out of White Creek Station bound for Chicago. Family and friends lined the platform, waving at the faces peering from the fogging windows and blowing their last kisses of the evening to the soon departed. Gaining speed, the train grew smaller and smaller in the twilight sky, eventually disappearing from sight. Soon, the wheels clacking on the track and the last whistles faded away into silence. The people left at the station stared a few moments longer and then one by one turned back to their lives and walked toward the exit.

Jordan stayed staring at the empty tracks for a few more moments before turning to leave. In the warm August evening, he felt a small tear fall and mix with the sweat streaming down his face. The humid air made his shirt sticky and the still night felt stifling. He wasn't looking forward to going home alone. He wiped the back of his hand across his face and turned away from the tracks. Sighing, he took a glance around and headed to the door to the parking lot.

The platform cleared out quicker than Jordan expected and realizing he was the only person left, he found the eerie silence disconcerting. As he was reaching his hand out to the exit, he stopped. A thumping echoed out through the empty station. Spinning around, he looked over at the ticket booth and found a blind pulled down behind the counter's bars with large bold face letters reading, 'CLOSED'. The lights inside were off and the platform lights flickered once, and with a loud humming, shut off plunging him into near darkness.

He moved back against the door. A click sounded out and the green emergency flood lights eerily illuminated the platform. Jordan started to open the door again to the stairwell when he heard the distinct sound of footsteps behind him. Slowly turning, he saw a man near the platform's edge looking back and forth.

Even in the humid night, he wore a dirty tattered trench coat and a faded ball cap. A pair of filthy and ragged red Converse high-tops completed the unsettling ensemble. Sniffing, the stranger lifted its head to the air and stared up at the starlit night sky. Brushing his long stringy blonde hair back off his shoulders, the figure fell to his knees bowing his head. His hands moved around the ground and Jordan saw him draw a large circle and fill it in with lines and random looking shapes. Tossing the chalk to the side, he pulled a folded piece of paper from his pocket and slowly unfolded it. Jordan could tell his hands were shaking badly and the paper almost fell from the stranger's grasp.

After the stranger cleared his throat, Jordan heard him begin to read something he didn't understand. Jordan felt like he was imposing on a private moment, but couldn't draw his eyes away.

"*Pater tenebris, exaudi orationem meam. Revertere illis qui amissa sunt, et eos, qui numquam inveni. Et sacrificium tibi sanguinis huius partem mecum. Sacra imperium terrae iniuriam Tu ad me recta habet et liberaret eos qui in custodia terrae,*" the man's voice chanted, his voice low and hypnotic.

Digging into his pocket, the man pulled out a knife and with a loud click he flicked the blade out of the handle. He tilted it back and forth in the flood lights and beams reflected from the shiny silver blade. Laying his hand on the floor, he drove the blade into his finger and began to saw his middle finger. Grunting, he tugged on the digit and the last of the tendons ripped free. Jordan recoiled and his hand flew up to cover his mouth from the acidic taste of vomit rocketing up from his stomach. He wanted to run away, but the ritual made him curious. After every album he'd listened to and every book he'd read, a real life ritual was being performed right before his eyes.

He couldn't turn away.

The torn page fluttered away from him and blew around the train station. Hurriedly, the man stumbled to his feet and ran the flying paper down. Grabbing by the edge of the track, he stuffed it back in his pocket and rushed back to the circle he drew on the platform.

In the distance, a train whistle called out in the night. Clouds swept through the sky and the moon's rays became blanketed by the growing darkness. The low chugging of an engine came rumbling from the west. Slowly, the momentum built and Jordan felt the ground shake the closer it came. The whistle screamed out again and the sound it emitted reminded him of a dying bird, a shriek sounding like it was crying in agony. Jordan felt exposed standing in the open by the door. He knew there were no other trains scheduled for the night; he and Cara chose the last one so they could be together for as long as possible. He wanted to know what this last train was coming for. Noticing a row of vending machines to the right, Jordan cautiously slunk over and hid in the shadows between them and the wall.

The man on the platform glanced back over his shoulder. Jordan froze in his tracks and his eyes locked with the dirty man. A knowing look was in the old man's eyes, and he turned away from Jordan.

"Go away boy, nothing for you here!" he called out and pressed his hand against his pant leg, the blood pooling at his feet from the severed finger. The green emergency lights made the blood look black against the floor.

A blinding light lit up the station and the train finally reached the platform. The dark train stopped with a deafening hiss and lurched to a halt in front of the man. Luminous inky smoke belched from the smokestack. Jordan stared transfixed on the bizarre train before him. The black finish looked shiny like a smooth piece of onyx and blood red highlights criss-crossed the cars to set the panels off from the rest of the train. Skeletons hung in chains from the train's cars and skulls adorned the engine's roof. Dark scarlet curtains covered the windows and pale yellow light escaped around the edges giving the train an unearthly glow.

Large plumes of steam erupted from the brakes on the old style steam engine and a squat man stepped from between the engine and the coal car. Jordan squinted to get a better look, and huffed in frustration at the dim green light. He couldn't tell for sure, but the shape standing between the man and the train looked like a dwarf. The small figure wore a bright red suit and a black hat topped off his uniform.

"Did you summon me?" the dwarf leered, and cackled a hoarse unholy laugh.

"Yes, I beg you to grant me my greatest desire," the man answered, his voice beaten and soulless.

"Do you have the required payment for the wish you summon me to grant?" he inquired and held out his tiny clawed hand.

The dirty man held out his hand and dropped his severed finger into the dwarf's palm. The conductor glanced down at it, pursed his lips and shook his head. He brought the offering to his lips, sniffing at the bloodied finger, and popped it in his mouth, swallowing it whole.

"Your sacrifice is most delicious, but for what you ask of me, I require more than just a finger," he said delightfully smacking his lips.

"I brought you my blood, a part of me for them!" the man cried out. Pain and rage filled his voice, but Jordan also caught a tone of fear and regret.

"The price is high for this wish, I require more," the conductor stated and climbed back aboard the train. Pulling the levers and firing up the furnace again, he turned back to the man.

"Once you have a more suitable gift, summon me and I will grant you your desire," he said and tugged on the whistle's chain.

The train began to move and the whistle blew its evil call into the night. Chugging along, the cars picked up speed and raced un-naturally fast from the station. In only a moment, the black train vanished in the night. The man dropped to his knees within the circle and sobbed.

Jordan slipped out from vending machines shadow and approached the hunched over man. His body shook from the weeping and Jordan reached out hesitantly, placing his hand on the man's shoulder.

"Are you ok?" he asked with concern in his voice.

"You shouldn't have stayed, son," the man looked up from his hands and said, smears of blood and tears on his checks.

"What was that?"

"I tried to get something I'd lost returned to me. Every day, their memories haunt me and I only wanted them back," he muttered and pulled a picture from his coat pocket. Jordan glanced over at the old faded photo in his hand. A cleaner, younger version of the man on the ground sat on a couch surrounded by Christmas presents and two young boys sat on either side of him snuggling in his side. All three looked happy and carefree.

"One day, I woke up and their little smiling faces weren't there any longer, my ex took them away from me. The bitch took my sons and I never saw them again. My heart feels like it'd been ripped from my chest. I've spent years trying to find a way to get them back again, and here I am." The man trailed his bloody stump along the boys' faces in the picture.

Jordan didn't know how to respond so he stayed silent.

"I only want to hold their tiny hands again and see the way they smiled with an innocence only a child can have," he said and turned toward Jordan, "but time eats away all life eventually."

"Well, I... I'm sorry man," Jordan murmured and took a step back.

"Nothing you could have done, son. Name's John by the way," the old man said and his head dropped defeated down on his chest as he stared down at the platform at his knees. Jordan glanced at the symbol on the floor and the pentagram within the circle made him curious. Other symbols and words adorned the picture and he got a chill up his spine just looking at it.

"Say, what're the marks on the floor for?" Jordan asked, his interest piqued.

John reached in his pocket and pulled out the yellowed page. The page was wrinkled and the paper began to tear along the old fold lines. Slowly, he raised it up and stared at the text swimming around on the page.

"To bring back what was lost, to summon the one who can fill the hole in my heart," John muttered and quickly shoved it back in his pocket. His palms slowly spread across the ground in front of him, and started to draw new lines in the circle.

Jordan took another step back. This guy just didn't seem quite right in the head. John's head turned toward him at the sound, and his bloodshot eyes blazed. Not liking the new look in the old man's eye, Jordan decided it was time to head out. Taking one more step backwards, Jordan spun and sprinted for the exit. Footfalls sounded out behind him as he yanked the door open. Jordan pulling the door shut and ran down the steps to the parking lot, flinging his car door open as he reached it. Gunning the engine, he tore out of the lot, spewing gravel behind him. Glancing in the rearview mirror, the last thing he saw before turning the corner onto Laymon Road was John standing by the doors.

Even speeding away, Jordan could still make out a slow smile spreading on John's face and the cold gaze in his eyes.

***

After he got off his latest call with Cara, he reclined back in his apartment and thought about the crazy guy from the train station two weeks ago. Something about the whole scene never sat well with him and the entire surreal incident had become lodged in his mind. He mentioned it to Cara, but she laughed it off, and told him he was creating a ploy to distract himself from being upset about her leaving for school. Admittedly, her being in Chicago and him being stuck in White Creek did frustrate him. She got to go try a new life, while he got left behind in their small hometown, alone. He couldn't stop thinking about it.

To bring back what was lost, to summon the one who can fill the hole in my heart.

Those words had bounced around the recesses of Jordan's mind since that night.

I wonder if John still goes to the station at night? He thought, sighing.

Getting up and walking around his apartment, settling down for lonely evening alone, he glanced longingly at Cara's picture on his bookshelf. Through his half-open drapes, he noticed the sun beginning to descend for the evening.

To bring back what was lost...

Deciding to act on the impulse, Jordan snatched his keys off the table and hurried out the door.

The station would be closing soon.

***

The last train goers were filing out of the station when Jordan arrived and hurried in before the closing time. Even though the station platform was open air, the main doors locked from the outside when the last train rolled out and the workers left to go home. The last custodian looked up as Jordan jogged by.

"Hey boy! The station is closing, so get moving!" the old man bellowed at Jordan.

Turning around, Jordan stopped for a moment and stared at the man in the gray coveralls before looking around for anyone else that could be in hiding. Shaking his head and muttering under his breath about this generation, the custodian returned back to his work sweeping the floor. The dirty broom swooshed slowly back and forth as he moved along, finishing his nightly tasks.

Jordan slid slowly over to the line of vending machines and backed into the shadows from the night before. Closing his eyes, he waited until he heard the footfalls fade away and the door lock latch a few moments later. Sticking his head around the corner of the dented Coke machine, the platform remained empty. A breeze blew through and various ticket stubs, candy wrappers, and newspaper pages fluttered around the station.

Maybe the guy isn't coming. I'm stupid for even coming back here anyway; he thought and plopped down on the floor.

Thirty minutes ticked by slowly and still the man hadn't made an appearance. Boredom started setting in and he started reaching for his phone to pass the time, when the first steps echoed in the empty station. Quickly scrambling to his feet, he looked out toward the tracks. The custodian came shuffling to the platform's edge, sat down, and tossed a paper sack next to him. He scooted closer to the end and threw his legs over the edge. Jordan heard his feet kicking against the concrete wall like a child.

"You can come out, son," the raspy voice called out. Jordan recoiled, a little sheepish that he was found out.

"How'd you know I was still here?"

"I knew you'd come back," the custodian answered and snorted a small laugh.

"You knew I'd come back?" Jordan curiously asked, walking to the platform's edge.

"I asked him for it and he granted it to me as a sign."

"John?" Jordan questioned, a cold knot formed in his gut.

"He decided to let me have something for my finger, and gave me a sign that you'd find me here," he cackled and held up his hand. A dark crimson bandage was wrapped around the stub where his middle finger used to be. Even two weeks later, blood still seeped through the crude bandage and dripped into his palm.

In the distance, a train whistle howled and the demonic sounding engine roared toward the White Creek Station, its screeching growing louder and louder. The high-pitched cries from the train made Jordan's ears hurt and he covered them with his fists. John knelt and started to redraw the symbols on the floor.

The first flash from the engine's headlamp flooded the platform and the sudden burst of light blinded Jordan. Below him on the floor, John laughed maniacally and drew faster. Jordan looked at him and saw the picture in the middle of the pentagram.

"Why are you doing this?" Jordan implored, too entranced to move away against his better judgment.

"Why? I want to hold those little boys in my arms one more time. I want to have what has been taken from me!" he roared at Jordan. Holding the page up, he waved it around frantically. "This can bring lost things back to you. I want it to bring my sons back!"

Jumping to his feet, John looked fiercely at him. His eyes were glazed and the dark circles underneath them looked like he hadn't slept in weeks. Nostrils flaring, he leaned in closer.

"I never spent the time with them I needed to and when I would be able to, they were gone!" he bellowed.

Jordan watched John shove the page in his pocket, its corner hanging halfway out. Jordan didn't want to stay, but his own need compelled him to try.

If only I can get it, I can make Cara come back to me; he thought and stepped closer to John.

Behind them, the menacing locomotive screeched to a halt. Insanity glared back at Jordan through John's eyes. Since the last time Jordan had seen the train, the angles twisted further out, perverting the train's original shape. Spikes stuck out from the top and severed heads rested on each, their mouths open in a silent scream. Bones replaced many of the rails and levers along the train's side and the bellowing smoke stank of sulfur and rot.

The conductor scuttled down from the engine and made his way to the platform, his feet never touching the floor.

"Ah, John I see your first request has been granted," the diminutive demon quipped.

John's head swung around and grinned gleefully at the conductor. Bending over, he picked the old faded picture up and held it up in the air. The impish conductor rose higher in the air and studied the picture closely.

"I can grant you your desire," he implied, his lips stretched further in the largest smile Jordan had ever seen, exposing the conductors bloodied gums and razor sharp black and rotted teeth.

"My sons?"

"Yes! Here, look into the first car and tell me what you see," the conductor said and waved his hand at the first car's scarlet velvet curtains. Untouched, they slid apart and inside bright multi-colored lights filled the car.

Jordan and John stared in the car in awe. In the back sat a Christmas tree and presents with shiny paper and satin bows surrounded the bottom. A brown couch ran along the far side and two young boys bounced up and down on the cushions. Their round faces grinned and each small boy giggled uncontrollably. Jordan remembered the worn photo John had shown him and the car matched it perfectly.

John fell to his knees and wept. Jordan stepped closer and the sight in the train car amazed him. He glanced back and spied the evil dwarf's satisfied look. Hearing something beside him, he turned as John rose up and dove at the train. In midair, he slammed into something invisible and bounced off, landing hard on the floor in the middle of the circle he drew.

"No, no, no John, you haven't paid fully yet," the conductor taunted and cackled.

"I'm prepared to pay, Conductor," John whimpered pitifully, his voice trailing off.

Jordan stood there and watched the scene. Out of the corner of his eye, he saw a page fall from John's pocket and drifted towards the platform. John slowly stood up, bloody hand on his knees, and shook his head as if he was trying to clear it in a daze.

The page! Jordan thought and made his way quickly to the circle. If John was going to get on the train tonight for his sons, Jordan needed to get the pages before he was gone.

As Jordan took the last step towards him, John moved back unexpectedly. As he backed away from the circle, Jordan slid into the chalk symbol ring to take his place. The boy's hand grabbed the page and he stood, a triumphant look on his young face.

"Sorry man, but I need to see my girl again," he snickered toward John.

Jordan turned and started to read through the old faded words. Digging in his pocket, he felt the bulge from the switchblade he'd brought with him. He grabbed a hold of the knife, pulling it out to begin his own ceremony.

Before he could act on his own, there was a blur of movement, and Jordan's knife was no longer in his hand. His stomach pounded as he suddenly looked up into John's maniacal grin. John's arm was thrust out and a spreading burning sensation rushed through Jordan's chest. Jordan's legs no longer wanted to support him, and he grabbed onto John's arm. Feeling a wet spray across his face, Jordan's head dropped, taking in the silver blade slowly being drawn back out of his gut. Blood poured out and rivets began running down his legs. He watched it flow onto the floor and slowly spread across John's symbol.

The conductor lightly landed on the platform and waddled over to the circle.

"Oh yes, this is nice. John, your wish is now paid in full," he said as he leaned down, wiping his finger through the pooling blood and licking it off.

Jordan felt the world spin, and losing his balance he fell to his knees as John let go of his arm. Before him, John climbed aboard the train and rushed toward the two beaming toddlers. He opened his arms wide and embraced the blond haired boys, sobbing loudly. Through his increasingly blurry vision, Jordan watched the boys open their mouths wide and start ripping John apart, his cries turning to screams. The little boys glanced up from their father's tattered throat and grinned before continuing to devour John.

The conductor leaned over and locked eyes with Jordan. He sniffed around his gore covered tee shirt and took another long lick of the blood drenched cotton.

"You are quite the tasty sacrifice," he whispered into Jordan's ear, his foul breath blowing in his face.

The train roared and a black mist crept from the engine's furnace and flowed out onto the platform. Jordan fell the rest of the way to the platform and rolled on his back, a darkness seeping into his vision. His body felt cold and the mist rolled over him, wrapping him up in its embrace.

Deep inside, his heartbeat slowed and the mist lifted his body into the air. His pores burned as the mist split into tiny tendrils and seeped in his body. They branched in his arms and legs, each tendril spreading deeper within him.

Jordan screamed in agony as he arched his back and closed his eyes. Withdrawing slowly, the mist hung in the air for a moment and suddenly was ripped out of Jordan's body. A bluish-white smoke followed the mist from his open mouth and the furnace roared again. With a loud cry, the blue-white mass flew into the furnace and the fire inside exploded in a blast of hellish heat as Jordan's body went limp.

The train's black chains whipped around his soulless corpse, and carried it to the side of the engine. The blistering heat from the furnace seared his flesh to the black iron, charring the boy's body as the latest eternal edifice of the train.

The conductor stepped into the blood tinged symbol and muttered an incantation to himself. The bloody chalk circle glowed a fiery orange and faded into the old dingy floor. A slow broken grin took his face as he peered over the new adornments on his train. Rising in the air, he drifted towards the controls and fired up the engine's furnace once more.

On the quickly darkening platform, the train pulled out and vanished, on to the next waiting station and the next waiting soul.

***

STORY NOTES:

This story sprang into my head one night and the impish conductor refused to go away until I wrote about him. While it takes place in White Creek, I only intended it to be loosely connected to the larger narrative about the town. In the end, I think the story really is about how I sit back and watch my sons growing up. The two boys in the story are the little kids I wish I could hold and snuggle again. If I had the ability to have that time back, what would I do? A piece of John is me speaking out about the boys leaving the nest. And Jordan? He's me too. There is a lot in this story about me...

BRENT ABELL

CALVARY HILL

The blazing sun began its western decent as Caleb McGowan rode in toward town. He halted his horse and his hardened eyes stared out at the setting twilight sky. The reds, oranges, and purples coloring the clouds were the only peaceful thing Caleb ever stopped to enjoy, especially while trying to stay one step in front of the law. Usually when he blew into a town, he'd also play some cards, drink some whiskey, and take on a whore or two, but nothing compared to the beauty the setting sun brought. He stroked his scruffy beard and chuckled to himself when he thought back to the night in Santa Fe when he paid for the whole whorehouse for himself and his now dead partner Jim Cullen. When the time came, he really hated putting him down, but it was either Jim or himself, so he put the bullet in Jim's head ensuring his escape from the U.S. marshals.

Caleb fled into the desert hoping they would never be able to find him. If he could get to the coast, he planned to board a ship headed for the Orient. Most outlaws hightailed it down to the old Mexico trail, but that was where the law always looked first. Caleb thought himself to be a cut above the other outlaws and figured the border was where all the bounty hunters and lawmen would look. Nope, he was going to be smooth and take to the ocean from California. A new world existed over the sea and he meant to start over. He patted the saddle bags full of gold coins from his last heist and rode on into the sunset.

After about an hour of riding, he spied a speck of light in front of him, about a half mile in the west. He slowed his horse to a trot and drew his pistol. He nervously flicked the hammer on the back of the Colt .45 and he drew nearer to the light not knowing what to expect. In the desert at night, a light could be used to distract a party while someone else robbed them from behind. He should know, he'd only pulled it off about twelve times in the past year.

When he was within sight of the light source, he saw a couple of torches blazing in the twilight. He drew closer till he was within spitting distance and hesitated. Caleb recognized the shape of a horse drawn hearse parked up on a little hill in the center overlooking the small cemetery. He urged his horse up to the gates and stopped. He holstered his gun and climbed down from the saddle. Once on the ground, he adjusted the brim of his hat and looked down. A scorpion scurried over to his boot. He raised his boot heel up and drove it down into the scorpion, squashing it's insides on the sides of his boot. He wiped his foot back and forth in the sand to clean it off and he spit his chew down on the dead scorpion's remains. He looked up at the arch that adorned the gate to the bone yard.

"Calvary Hill, huh," he muttered to himself while passing underneath the arch. He rubbed the deep knife scar on his cheek as he made his way through the cemetery.

A voice came calling down from the hearse, "Who goes there? I'm armed!"

Caleb placed his hand on the butt of his gun and proceeded to walk up to the gravedigger.

"I said who goes there damn it!"

Caleb silently stalked around behind the hearse and found himself looking at the young gravedigger's back. He flipped the leather strap of the holster's top, freeing his gun should he need to draw quickly. Taking another step, he heard the crunch of dead weeds beneath him. The boy turned and swung the shovel in Caleb's direction, but he was too slow. Caleb's hand pulled up fast and while ducking the wild swinging arc of the shovel, stuck the gun barrel in the boy's face. His thumb pulled back the hammer and he cleared his throat.

"Best you drop the digger now, boy," his voice cold and hollow.

"Yes sir, just don't kill me," the boy stammered as the shovel handle quickly slid from his grasp and fell to the ground. Caleb laughed a little at this. The boy was barely old enough to leave home or shave, as his light brown stubble could attest. The rest of his face looked as smooth as the day he was born.

"How far is town?"

"Calvary Hill? It's only a ten minute ride from here."

"Any law there?"

"Just one sheriff and a few deputized men."

"How big is the town?"

"Oh, only about forty people sir. You could say we are the ass of the desert. All the waste collects in town and ends up in the graves here. There's a saloon, a hotel, and a jail. I guess we could pass as a town out here in this God forsaken hell hole."

Caleb dropped the gun down from the boy's head since he didn't seem to be much of a threat. Calvary Hill sounded like the kind of place he could stay a couple of days, win some more cash, and then finish out his ride to the coast.

"So, what brings you to this part of the desert?" The boy asked after a moment when he was sure he wouldn't be shot. His bright blue eyes studied Caleb's facial scars and the iron strapped at his side. He picked the shovel back up and he threw some dirt into the freshly dug grave, eyeing Caleb the whole time.

"Making my way to the border and then into ol' Mexico." He lied, not knowing if the law would ever end up here questioning the boy.

"You're headed the wrong way then mister. Only thing out this way is nothing. Border is south anyway, so if you need a compass I could sell you one," the boy said, still filling the hole.

"Maybe I'll just ride into town and spend a day or so. Runnin' low on cash anyway, so some cards will do." Caleb sniffed the air and wrinkled his nose. Perhaps it was because he was close to one of the torches, but he could smell fire and it had a different twang than what he was used to.

"Do you need a guide to town?" The boy asked as he patted down the sandy dirt on top of the grave. Caleb noticed that he was very careful not to step on the grave when he circled it to put the shovel back onto the hearse. "I can show you around and I might be able to help you on your way. Everyone needs a hand every now and again." He winked at Caleb and smiled.

"I guess I could let you show me around," Caleb said. He turned and strolled back through the grave markers to the gate. As he passed them, he glanced down at the names painted on the worn wooden crosses. In most instances, he could make out parts of names and when they died. He wouldn't normally give a damn about the town folk, but it didn't escape his notice that the death dates all seemed to be within a five year period.

"Noticed the markers, huh?"

"A lot are close to the same dates."

"Shit happens? Let's get to town so I can show you around while we still have some light. The Venus Hotel fills up when the cards and liquor run out at Milton's Saloon. Name is Dante, by the way," the boy said over his shoulder as he hopped up on to the hearse carriage. He grabbed the reigns and urged the horse down to the cemetery gate.

"Aren't you even going to ask why I'm runnin'?"

"Ok, I'm game. Why are you runnin' for the border?"

Caleb thought the kid couldn't do anything to him if he did know and when drunk he would brag about it any chance he would get. "I've killed thirty-five people in three territories over the last few years. Since the war, I left the south and decided to stake me a claim out here. Well, after a bad run at the tables, I had to stake my claim as a bank robber. My claim is good too."

"Sounds like you have been a very bad man. It might be interesting to hang around you for a spell."

"Well, I say let's ride so that I get in town by full dark and have some fun." Caleb was already saddling up as pulled his duster tightly around him. The desert air took on a biting chill and it cooled with each passing minute.

Caleb waited for Dante to lead the hearse out and he fell in line behind. His gut hurt. It was not a too-much-whiskey-and-whoring-hurt, but the something-doesn't-feel-right-hurt. He decided to ignore it; the call of what was to come took over. Caleb followed through the desert and the cacti. He heard the buzzards still circle as they searched for one last meal before the sun was gone for the chilly darkness of the night. They circled the riders and flew off toward their nest with nothing to show their young for their efforts.

***

The ride took about twenty minutes and the darkness finished consuming the land by the time they reached the edge of town. Caleb thought it looked like every other middle of nowhere town throughout the Texas and New Mexico territories. The town was one large dirt lane with businesses and the town government buildings lining both sides. Behind each main building was a secondary pass up each side where small residential dwellings where located. Each one appeared as a dilapidated construction with flapping canvas for roofs and cast off wood for sides. When Caleb rode by the ones closest to the town's gates, he could hear the muffled cries of young children inside.

Dante pulled the hearse to a stop in front of a brightly lit saloon. He motioned for Caleb to come closer as he dismounted. Caleb moved next to Dante and slung himself from his horse, pulling his hat down to cover his eyes.

"Well, here we are. This is Milton's. Inside you'll find a mess of folk who want to gamble, drink, and on occasion shoot 'em up. The dealer is a cheat and Milton waters down the whiskey, but there ain't a lot of choice around here I'm afraid."

"This will do nicely. So where can I hitch up Buck here and grab a room for the night?"

"The Venus is up the way a couple of buildings. Nobody really stays there though. Most people here either live in the shanties or they just sleep where they passed out. Milton allows that kinda thing, but he may pick your pockets while you're out."

"Well, I reckon I'll hit the saloon first and see where the night takes me," Caleb said. He began to laugh and turned to walk up the front stairs to the saloon. Dante followed close behind.

Caleb came to the swinging doors and pushed them open gently so he wouldn't raise a ruckus when he entered. It went against his style, because when he held up a stagecoach or a bank, he would just kick the door in. He thought about the burning he felt in his gut earlier and he wondered if that helped to foster his hesitancy. Out of habit, he flipped off the leather straps from the top of his holsters and strolled over to the bar.

The barkeep saw Caleb belly up to the bar and was over to him quickly. "What can I get ya' this evening?"

"Whiskey, and hold the water," Caleb said as he took a seat on the stool.

"Your guns, you'll have to check them in. No shootin' in here I'm afraid," said the barkeep as he gazed down at Caleb's Colts. Dante came over to the bar and stood beside Caleb.

"He's fine John, he can keep his guns," stated Dante. There was an edge in his voice and demeanor that Caleb hadn't heard at the cemetery. At the sound of Dante's voice, John turned, poured Caleb a shot, and walked away.

Caleb threw back the shot and welcomed the burning sensation rushing down his throat and into his gut. He ordered another and headed over to the card table. Six men and a dealer sat in a circle around the table engaged in a hand of poker. Caleb spied an open seat opposite the dealer and sat down. Two whores moved over to him and brought him another drink plus some poker chips. After dropping their wares in front of him, they began hanging on each side of him, each one positioning herself to be the one keeping his bed warm later in the night. He reached over and patted their behinds and beckoned them closer to him.

"Do whom do I owe the pleasure of the chips and your company?"

"Dante paid for us, the drink, and the chips. He said to enjoy." They each kissed him on the check and then kissed each other. They looked up at Caleb and licked their lips. There was something familiar about them, but he couldn't seem to put his finger on it.

The dealer cleared his throat to get Caleb's attention. Caleb threw his ante into the pot and waited for his cards. The dealer double checked the pot and proceeded to deal. Caleb was checking over his cards and felt the eyes of the table on him. He glanced up and noticed everyone staring at him. He stopped and stared back, his free hand already dropping down below the table. Just like the whores, the men and the dealer seemed vaguely familiar also. It unsettled him that these people acted like they knew him, because he had no idea who the hell they were.

Caleb threw his bet into the pot after he stopped glaring at the other gamblers and brought his draw hand back to the table's top. He was sweating even though the temp inside was cold. Caleb laid his hand down and pulled his duster tighter around him. When he moved, he noticed three of the men flinch towards their holsters. Caleb realized everyone was still armed, the bartender let everyone keep their irons. *This was going to be an interesting game*, Caleb thought.

By the fourth hand, tempers were growing short around the table. Three of the men had already begun to accuse Caleb of cheating. He was taking it rather well, because usually the first man to do it ended up eating a bullet either at the table or in the street like a dog. At one point or another, each man had the twitch, the need to draw and protect their honor. The fifth hand started like all the rest until the man next to the dealer opened his mouth.

"I think that this man who has joined us is a liar and a cheat. So help me on my family's name," he said. His voice became more agitated.

"Gerald, watch what you say," cautioned the man next to him.

The name Gerald screamed in Caleb's mind. A realization stuck him as the clouds opened up outside in rain and thunder, the lightning flashing throughout the saloon. Gerald Hume, a man he gunned down in El Paso sat across from him. The whores he killed as cover escaping from Santa Fe. The faces of the other men around the table clicked in his memory. They were all men he put in the ground in the past five years.

As realization dawned on his face, the saloon crowd started to surround the table, blocking Caleb's escape route. The whores tried to grab him and the people were two and three deep leaving him no place to run. He glanced back over to Gerald and gasped. The normal face he had been watching playing cards began to shift, the color fading to an ashen gray. The wound from the shot he took to the temple opened and began to run with blood and pus. Caleb drew both Colts and jumped up from his chair, kicking it backwards. He frantically waved his guns back and forth, side to side watching in horror as the wounds manifested on everyone in the saloon. They were familiar because he had done this; these wounds were caused by his hands, and his guns. A loud clapping sounded from the bar area. Caleb swung himself in that direction and saw that Dante was standing on top of the bar applauding the scene playing out.

"Very good, very good. Please back away from our guest. Sheriff, please take his irons from him and bind his hands," Dante ordered.

The sheriff, Caleb recognized as someone he gunned down in the Arizona badlands, approached him. Caleb put the barrels to the lawman's head and pulled the trigger. The lawman's face disintegrated in a shower of blood and bone fragments, splashing the wall behind him. The lawman still stood there, hands outstretched waiting for Caleb to relinquish his guns. Caleb pushed on the corpse, seeing if it would fall over. The body stood firm. Beaten and seeing no way out, Caleb handed over his Colts to the now headless sheriff. He grabbed them from his hands and tossed them to Dante, still perched on top of the bar. The sheriff pulled out a rope and bound Caleb's hands together, making sure he pulled the rope extra tight so it would bring the pain.

"What is the meaning of this?" Caleb yelled out Dante. Dante turned and smiled.

"My name is Dante Morningstar and I have heard the cries of revenge from these people. You are a very wicked man indeed, Mr. McGowan, and I wanted to harvest you personally." He jumped down from the bar and headed towards Caleb, the people clearing a path for him.

"Harvest?"

"I have followed your career with much interest, my friend. You have created a path of death that made the Reaper jealous. These were just the few out of hundreds you killed who would give me their souls to watch you suffer and my did their suffering attract me to the surface. The blood you spilled and the women you raped attracted me to your soul. All good things must end however, and you have reached the end of your line." Dante turned to the people and said, "Go now and prepare the gallows noose. I promised you he would hang for his crimes against you and I never break my word."

The people filed out, except the sheriff, Dante, and Caleb. The sheriff pushed Caleb back down into the chair and pointed a gun to his temple.

"Now, now my friend, we must not rob the town of their revenge. I will allow you to take out some anger over the gut shot that killed you however."

The now headless sheriff took the butt of his gun and started to pistol whip Caleb. After about ten minutes, he was out cold and by then the gallows were almost complete.

***

When Caleb awoke, everything was still dark. He could feel the rough burlap covering his face and he sweating in the sweltering mask. Caleb wondered how long he'd out cold. He could feel the prickling heat from the torches on his exposed flesh where he stood. His ears could hear the shuffling of the townsfolk and the cries from the vultures circling overhead. Turning his head, he felt the frayed rope around his throat. Caleb tapped his boot down and felt out the stool top he was placed on.

"Shit," he muttered to himself.

He heard some more commotion to his left, someone was approaching him. He felt hands take hold of the burlap sack and rip it from his head. Caleb squinted when the firelight blasted his corneas. Blinking, he could make out the gates of the cemetery. Scanning the scene in front of him, he saw that thirty-five people stood before him. Their eyes were blank and all held their gaze at Caleb. He closed his eyes to block out the images of the flesh hanging from the dead. Caleb knew this was it and he tried to make his peace with the Lord, but the moaning of guilt radiated from the crowd like the noonday's sun's heat on the trail. The sounds of shoveling dirt assaulted his hearing from the right. Dante looked up and waved at him.

"Just getting your place ready Caleb. You can rest with those you put here. I even have a surprise for you Caleb. You hear that, it's your lucky day, I brought a friend with me who is dying to see you again!" Dante hollered and dug a little more. "You know, I could have someone or something else do this for me, but I really like to get my hands dirty. Nothing beats digging a fresh grave before you throw a body in it."

Caleb turned his head and tried to spit, but his mouth was dry from the desert heat. Another vulture cried out in anticipation, wanting to eat. The crowd cheered as Dante emerged from the hole and slammed his shovel down into the dirt pile.

"It is done. I will now let you have your vengeance, for I am the Morningstar!" Dante started to change. His body elongated and his clothes started to smoke. The tint of his skin darkened to a deep red and his clothes burst into flames and burned off his body. He stood over seven feet tall and looked out lovingly over the assembled crowd. His flesh hardened and rippled as scales replaced the skin. Caleb couldn't turn away as he watched the transformation before him. Dante's head split on both sides as pointed horns emerged from his skin and broke out from his skull. A ripping sounded as his tail tore through the skin on his back and whipped out towards Caleb. Caleb held firm and didn't blink as Dante moved closer to him. When they were looking face to face, Caleb called forth enough spit to send flying out into Dante's face.

"I knew you would come for me eventually," Caleb said in a calm voice.

"When I came to your partner Jim as he lay dying, he told me he would give his soul to watch you when you died as did all these other lovely people. I wanted his soul, but I really wanted yours," Dante said as his voice trailed off into a hiss when he finished speaking.

A man in a black hood walked up to the gallows and stood beside Caleb. He reached up and tugged off his hood. Jim Cullen looked back at him. Like all the other dead, the single bullet hole he put there still festered in his forehead.

"I hoped I would see you hang, you son of a bitch," Jim said as he struck Caleb across the mouth. Caleb swished his mouth around and spit blood down on the ground.

"You can go screw yourself. I did what I had to do to get out of your mistake, so take your little black hood and go on now," Caleb spoke in defiance.

Dante pushed Jim back and spoke, this time he addressed the town. "All of you paid me for the opportunity to avenge your senseless deaths. Here he is, for all to see! Jim, if you would please."

Jim pulled his hood back down and in one swift motion, kicked the stool out from underneath Caleb's feet. The rope snapped around his neck as he fell, but it did not break his neck. He hung there, swinging and struggling to get free, his feet kicking in the air.

"My brothers and sisters, you may now partake of him!" Dante cried out to the crowd.

One by one, the crowd approached the gallows. When the first person reached Caleb, they reached up and grabbed his chest. Ripping the flesh off from Caleb's side, the man placed the flesh over the bullet hole in his body. Caleb watched as the flesh mended together, healing the wound and then the man disappeared from sight. Caleb screamed as one after another, the townsfolk come forwards and tore into his skin and muscles, each taking with them what they had lost. Every piece that was torn from him made him scream in agony. Pieces of his arms, his legs, and even his lungs were removed as each person tried to make themselves whole again. Thirty-four took from Caleb what they had lost, but Caleb saw that one more remained. The blood that remained in his veins turned to ice when he saw the last one. He whispered one last prayer, knowing it fell on deaf ears. The sheriff staggered forwards and felt for Caleb, because without the head Caleb had blown off in the bar, he couldn't see. Once he felt Caleb's legs he reached up and took hold of Caleb's head, twisting it to the right and left.

Dante Morningstar patted Jim Cullen on the shoulder. Jim smiled as the headless man twisted and turn, pulled and ripped, until the head was separated from Caleb's neck, the spinal cord swinging. Caleb's body slipped from the noose and fell to the ground, the last of his life blood pouring out onto the desert sand. The sheriff held the head and gently placed it on his neck, adjusting it until it stayed securely. He nodded to Dante as he faded into the night.

"Are you pleased?" asked Dante as he started to walk away from Jim.

"That was what I needed," he said to Dante, his gaze cast down to ground. He knew that now it was his time to pay. He felt the burning as his soul fled his body. He screamed out to God as the sand opened and chains flew up from Hell, dragging him down.

Dante kicked sand into the hole that swallowed Jim and laughed. Spreading his wings, he flew off into the approaching dawn.

***

Dante Morningstar returned with the hearse later in the evening and began his task of burying the dead. He took out the shovel and began to heap the earth back into the open grave. The dirt rained down on Caleb McGowan, covering his decapitated remains. Most of the flesh the townsfolk left on his bones became a feast for the circling buzzards. The sunset had fallen over the land and Dante stopped to take a break and unfurling his wings, gave them a stretch. Not far away, he heard the trotting of a horse creep closer to the cemetery. Slade Jackson was early in arriving to his judgment, but Dante would not deny him. He finished folding his wings into his back and hopped out of the hole he was filling in. Duty called and the Morningstar's work was never done.

***

STORY NOTES:

All I can say about his one is I sat around one night and thought about if Lucifer enjoyed his work and if he liked being a 'hands-on' kind of guy. This story also is my first dabble in the 'weird western' genre. It was fun and I liked the idea of a town where outlaws had to go to meet those they wronged and have them pass judgment with a little help from the Morningstar.

DO US PART

Harold kneeled down weeping in the newly fallen snow. The roses he brought yesterday already drooped to the ground; the wilted and frozen petals covering the area below the thorny stems. Running his gloved hand over the gravestone's etching, he whispered her name over and over like an incantation. Each time her name crossed his lips; he felt her inside him and imagined her touch again. When Valerie died, a piece of him died with her and he couldn't stand the empty house and bed any longer. Work had understood at first, but after not returning calls for a week they fired him earlier in the day while he lay in bed clutching her pillow and weeping. The only time he escaped the memory of Valerie was to come to her grave and grieve alone.

Shivering, Harold climbed to his feet, blew a kiss to the granite marker, and took another long pull from the whiskey bottle. The temperature continued dropping and the cold howling wind cut through his coat like a knife. Still he lingered above her resting place and prayed, not able to pull himself away from her side. Inhaling the frigid air deep into his lungs, he closed his eyes. With the world around him shut out, he prayed one last prayer and his mind wandered to the news he heard on the radio.

News reports of the dead rising flooded the airwaves over the last three days, but coming out here to see for his self was pitiful, the old him never would have even began to believe it, but things had changed. Death can change a man. The ludicrous notion the dead were coming back to life gave him hope he'd see Valerie again, but standing there he felt hope die like the day she was killed two weeks ago. Every day since the burial, he made the trek through the cemetery, flowers and bottle in hand, until he reached her sleeping remains. Now it felt different, like hope's beacon lit his path and called for him to seek her out again. He knew it was a fool's errand, but he wanted to give it one last go.

The scream he heard piercing the quiet December evening snapped him back to reality.

Beyond the mausoleum, another cry filled the air and cut short. Harold hurriedly stumbled to his feet and ran to the tree line on his left. Stopping, he heaved gasping for air and turned to look behind him. The cemetery's rolling hills were silent again and the swaying tree branches were the only thing moving. He stopped and a shadow crept out from behind one of the old crypts in the cemetery's center. The person's foot left crimson drag marks in the snow and he saw the foot twisted backward and a chunk of leg missing.

"Damn," he muttered under his breath and moved away from the crypts. Harold stopped to check his surroundings again and gasped. The snow betrayed his location, his tracks marking the white drifts, leading whatever was out there straight to him. Pausing for a moment, he scanned the area again.

The bushes beside the mausoleum rustled and two shapes crept out from the holly. Shambling, the figures moved to the road and their eyes roamed around scanning the ground. The female lifted her head and sniffed the air like an animal. Sensing something, the male inspected the ground. Dropping down on his hands and knees, he buried his nose in the snow and searched the area around him. Stopping at the footprint, he lifted his head and hissed. The female slowly made her way over to him and hissed back.

Harold froze in place. Even in the frigid evening air, cold perspiration dripped down his forehead. Hoping to stay unnoticed, he fought back the shivers and didn't move a muscle.

A dog limped toward him from the trees. Growling, the canine slowly approached him, dragging its back leg behind him. Hearing the commotion, the strangers turned and scanned the tree line. Looking down, Harold noticed the dog's paws were bloody and its belly was laid open leaving an intestinal trail behind.

Both took a step toward the trees. Striking with his foot, he kicked the dog over and carefully raised his foot. Slowly, as to not bring notice, he sat his foot on the dog's head and pushed with all his might downward into the frozen ground.

Bones cracked beneath his heel and the weird growling ceased. The other two things drew closer to his position and the time wasted on the dog left him no time to get away. The branch in front of him covered his body from view. Gradually, he lowered himself down and laid flat on the snow cover. Reaching out, he scooped snow with his arms and buried himself beneath the frozen blanket.

Bit by bit, the people shuffled next to him. Blood dripped from their mouths and drenched their tattered clothes. Harold noticed the skin on the man's hands peeled back and the bone shone through the fingertips. The fingernails were ripped off where they dug themselves out from somewhere deep in the winter ground. Crimson drops dotted the virgin white, contrasting in the last fading light. Deep in his bones, the winter evening and the snow blanket drained his strength. Struggling to focus, he clenched his jaw shut so his teeth didn't chatter and he lowered his breathing to a faint rise and fall of his chest.

Once his mind had a moment to process the situation around him, it hit him, *Oh my God, they are real. The news is right!*

Harold stayed buried for what he considered an eternity. The last sun rays bleed away to the coming night.

The stench wafting from the corpses crept up his nose and his gag reflex kicked in. Rolling over, he climbed up and turned around. The female body grinned at him and fresh chunks of meat fell to the ground from beneath her blackened teeth. Batting her eyelids over liquefied eyeballs, she cried out an unholy cry into the twilight. A chorus rose from all around the cemetery in response.

Harold ran. Feeling around in his pockets for anything he could use as a weapon, he found only keys, cell phone, and a napkin.

Then an idea hit him, *the whiskey bottle at the grave!*

Remembering the empty bottle he left at Valerie's grave, he sprinted to his salvation. Moans erupted all around him. The sun's last rays cast a hundred shadows around the fallen markers and the piles of dirt pushed up from below. The wind bellowed harder and the sounds of the other dead drew nearer to him. Arriving at Valerie's grave, he bent over to grab the bottle and froze.

The vase of roses lay toppled over, the displaced dirt thrown around the area where her body rested. A branch broke behind the large stone cross behind him. Guardedly, he rose and gripped the bottle tight in his bitterly cold hand. Out of time, Harold reared back with the bottle and brought it down on the granite marker. Glass exploded and he raised the broken bottle up like a knife. The mix of tension and icy temperatures left his hands frozen and white. Ducking down, he crouched behind her marker. Another branch broke and a figure emerged from the shadows.

Steps crunched in the snow and Harold hid, afraid of what awaited him. Gathering all his courage and all his hopes, Harold stood and was stunned.

Valerie's dress flowed behind her in the gale and the driving snow covered her gray flesh. Her dead body took another step and stopped. Her head turned to the side like she remembered him, a memory fragment from the living past. The bottle slipped from his grasp and he looked to the darkened sky, thanking those above for answering his prayers.

Arms wide open; she stepped closer and groaned. The noise meant nothing, but to him it meant everything. Tears froze to his cheeks and he smiled. To him she was still the most beautiful thing he'd ever laid eyes on.

"Valerie, I love you," he proclaimed and wrapped himself up in her embrace. He ran his hands over her back and cringed touching the cold flesh.

Heat rushed through his body and something he hadn't felt in weeks smoldered in him. Holding her in his arms again, he leaned in and gently pressing his lips to her blue cracked mouth, kissing her.

Harold backed away after tasting his wife's foul breath and gazed into her dead black eyes. She looked at him and cocked her head to the side, a low rumble coming from her gas filled stomach. The truth screamed in his head.

"You're dead. My God, what am I thinking?" he whispered to her and felt all hope fade.

Drawing closer again, he embraced her and kissed her throat where she used to like it before they made love. Feeling her freezing corpse again, he closed his eyes and gave her a quick kiss on her forehead. In the distance he heard the others nearing and made his choice. Harold backed away and pulled the heavy coat collar away from his neck. He dropped his arms and lifted his head to the heavens while Valerie approached him.

Welcoming her teeth in his throat, he closed his eyes knowing they'd be reunited in their love, together forever.

***

STORY NOTES:

I am terrible at saying goodbye and letting things go. The character in here is my attempt to sort out how I'd act if I became a widower. I only hope the zombie apocalypse doesn't start while I'm at the cemetery.

THE SLEEPER WAKES

Darrin awoke and rubbed his sore puffy eyes. Something seemed different; the vast nothing he saw every waking hour for the last six years was gone. Instead he found around the edges of his sight, light peeked in. Color slowly seeped in and continued to replace the black. His father promised him a cure every day since he went blind and today Darrin thought he finally succeeded.

Three days ago, his father brought him the first dose of something he'd been developing at work. Drinking the vile smelling liquid down brought results at first, he did see light, but the bright orbs quickly faded away within a few precious minutes. He told his father and they tried some quick tests to verify what was happening. His sight returned to complete darkness until his father gave him a bigger second dose before leaving for the lab earlier in the morning. Darrin hoped his father lived up to the promise he made, to help him see again and leave the darkness behind forever. He crawled back into bed and pulled the covers up over his head, hoping for a miracle when he awoke again.

After tossing and turning for a few hours after receiving the second dose, Darrin woke up and began to blink repeatedly, gradually clearing his vision and bringing the world into cloudy focus. Shapes and different hues sharpened until after six years of darkness, Darrin saw images again. Seeing was pretty much how he remembered it, except for a black speck in the center of his vision. He closed his eyes rapidly to make it go away, but it remained, hovering in midair in front of him.

He leaned his head back and closed his eyes. Squeezing them shut tightly, he kept them closed for a few minutes. Cautiously reopening his eyes, he saw the spot remained and had grown in diameter. Swinging his head back and forth he tried to shake free of the spot, but it stayed in the middle of his vision no matter fast and hard he turned his head.

Closing his eyes again trying to make the black place go away brought with it a new problem. In his head a droning echoed in his brain. He tried opening his eyes to see if it would stop, but the sound only grew louder. He focused on the noise and it reminded him of chanting. Screaming, his knees gave out beneath him and he fell to the floor. Curling up into a ball, Darrin whimpered in agony while waves of pain crashed in his head. Scared, he closed his eyes again and prayed his father would hurry home.

***

"Edward, I gave the M1-28 to Darrin."

Edward James reached over and grabbed John Clark by his lab coat and pulled him closer.

"You did what?" His hushed tone was pointed and hostile.

"Look, you of all people know I would do anything for Darrin and I couldn't wait for the ok to start trials in human subjects."

"I know, but your own son? Jesus Christ, what the hell were you thinking? Did you even consider the possible side-effects? Even if the M1 did work and gave Darrin his eyesight back, the method you used jeopardizes the whole thing! The FDA will crucify us and wait until the media and markets catch wind of it! We'll be ruined!" Edward exclaimed as he pulled John toward his office door.

"Edward, listen to me… it works," John subtly stated as the two doctors stepped inside Edward's office.

"What do you mean it works?" Edward asked as he sat down behind his desk and settled into his posh leather chair.

"Darrin has exhibited macular regeneration in his eyes. The first dose only produced a short-lived frame of sight. Once the drug cycled through his system, the blindness returned. After the second dose, a few hours later he came back down from his room and told me he could make out points of light in his vision which is impossible with his condition. I didn't believe him at first, but when I moved my hands in front of his face; his eyeballs moved slightly and followed my hand. We did that this morning before I left to come in here."

"Have you told anyone else?"

"No, why the hell would I do that? You're my partner and we developed that drug together."

"You have to bring him in for me to examine. I need to see for myself because if what you claim is true, we've got to study the effects on him."

"What Edward, you don't believe me?"

"No, no, I do, but I just have to make absolutely sure what you're telling me is what happened before we decide how to proceed with the findings and how we're going to break it to the FDA when they inquire about the unauthorized trial you performed on Darrin."

"Proceed?"

"Yes. How the hell would it look if we just stepped out announcing a drug that cures blindness and that we happened to test it on your son before human trials were approved by the FDA? If we don't get our story straight, it might look like jail for us. You're my friend and the best damned researcher I've ever worked with, but I'm not going to jail for you."

The two men sat across from each other at the desk and stared at each other. John was surprised by Edward's reluctance to going public and Edward was just as surprised by John's recklessness about going public. They were partners for fifteen years and the last six on the project started when four year old Darrin lost his sight to an overly aggressive macular degeneration. John threw his career on the line to work on a drug that would allow his son to see again.

"How many doses did you administer again?"

"It only took two doses before he started exhibiting sight regeneration."

"Bring him in now and don't say anything to anybody. If he really can see, tell him to fake still being blind. If too many people see him stroll through looking at things, some uncomfortable questions might be raised a little early."

John stood up and started to walk out. He turned around and looked at Edward, "I'll get him in here in a few hours so have the lab ready."

Edward leaned back in his chair and smiled, "let's see what we have here and then decide how we continue. Be back here in two hours. I'll sign the lab crew out and we should have it without interruption for the rest of the day."

John gave one last nod and walked out.

***

Darrin sat in his chair trembling. The searing pain subsided, but he still felt the dull throbbing in his skull. He saw things again, not the black nothing he'd been cursed with since the sickness, but he saw images. Everything he remembered about his sight didn't include the small black dot in the middle of his sight line. It still hovered in the center of everything he tried to look at. When he moved his head, it moved. If he closed his eyes, it disappeared, but came back as soon as he opened them back up again.

Years without sight gave him some reservations about the spot and he pondered if it would just go away. Rubbing his eyes again, he squinted trying to focus on the curtains on his windows. The bright red fabric still contained the black in the middle. It seemed different to Darrin. In fact, he thought it looked bigger than it did earlier in the morning.

A digital camera sat on his desk taunting him. His father left it in case he felt like snapping a few frames of his world, trophies to his returned sight.

I wonder if the spot shows up in pictures, Darrin wondered, his fingers brushing up and down the camera's side. Without thinking, he picked it up and quickly snapped a shot of the wall in front of him. He closely inspected the screen and failed to see the spot in the frame. To his chagrin, it remained only in his normal sight. Staring at the view screen, a low rumble filled his head.

Since he went back to sleep the static noise in his head grew louder. Mostly it sounded like an off-air television station with occasional gibberish words slipped in. The longer it went on, the more and more like chanting it became.

The sun began to descend and he sat gazing out the window. Every moment the spot grew until it covered Mr. Nelson's house next door. The edges were hazy and he couldn't focus anymore. Most of his central vision was now like an eclipse. The pounding in his head grew louder and now he knew the sounds were chants. Nothing he heard in his mind made any sense. The words sounded like the Latin he'd heard at Mass, but the vibe it gave off was… different. He tried to block them out, but nothing worked even when he jammed his fingers in his ears.

Darrin did the only thing seeming to help keep the spot from growing, he closed his eyes and waited.

***

"Darrin? Darrin? I'm home!" John called out when he opened the door to the house.

"Dad, up here in my room!" Pain and a fearful tremor filled his voice.

John tossed his coat on the stair railing and ran up to Darrin's room, his mind racing about the drug and the fear he heard in Darrin's voice. A gnawing hit him in the gut.

What if there were side-effects? Is he hurt? Does he know I did it because I love him?

The last thought hurt the most. John hoped his son loved him and knew if something went wrong it was only because he wanted to help him at any cost.

But what was the cost John? He heard Edwards voice in his head.

Swinging open the door, his heart sank at the sight of his son lying on the floor, curled into a fetal ball. Darrin looked up and John could make out the red streaks on his cheeks where he'd cried.

"You ok buddy?" John got down next to Darrin and asked.

"I can still see dad, but the spot blocks most of it."

"What spot?"

"When I open my eyes all I can see is a big black dot and it's growing bigger. My head hurts really bad too."

"Well, we're going to go see what we can do about it ok? Let me leave your mother a message and then I taking you to the lab," John said getting his phone out and texting Olivia.

"Will Uncle Edward be there?"

"Yep, but we need to hurry," John answered scoping Darrin off the floor.

Hurrying out to the car, John never noticed Darrin kept his eyes closed and mouthed the word, *'sleeper',* over and over again.

***

Edward already sat in the lab with their assistant Tony Gallardo by the time they arrived. Both sported lab coats and were setting up the CAT scan system running equipment tests.

"John, Darrin, how are you?" asked Tony.

"I'm not too good Mr. Gallardo," muttered Darrin sheepishly.

Tony patted him on the head trying to calm him down. "You know what we're going to do, right sport?"

"Dad just said guys were going to help me."

Edward stepped over and took Darrin by the shoulders, "we need to look at your brain and see what's going on in there. Once we see what your brain is up too, we can figure out how to help."

"Are you ready big guy?" John asked.

"Yeah, I am," Darrin said and bounded into his father's arms. Father and son embraced until Tony lead him into the examination room.

***

Tony finished tightening the wrist restraints on Darrin and stepped back. He gave a thumbs-up to John and Edward in the control room and he heard the hum of the scanner. Backing away, he sat in the secondary control room and finished powering up the machine.

Darrin lay on the table and kept his eyes tightly shut. He tried with everything he had to keep them shut so the spot would stop growing. It consumed almost all of his vision. The table he was strapped to shift and he grew fearful again. In his head the chanting for the *Sleeper,* drowned out the whir and whining as the gears slid him into the cavernous scan tube.

His father's soothing voice called out to him from the outside, "Darrin, we only need a few shots. I need you to relax, breathe easy, and hold still so we can get a good set of reading."

Releasing the breath he'd been holding since the machine started humming around him, he relaxed. The sounds from the machine did little to drown out the chants however. The voices grew louder and pounded in his skull like the beating of a drum.

"Dad! The voices are getting louder and they hurt!" Darrin cried out from the scanner.

In the control room, John reached over and pressing the intercom button, tried to calm him down. "Darrin, please relax and take steady breaths. We're starting to get the first readings now."

"John, look at this," Edward said pointing to the multicolored readout of Darrin's brain.

John looked and felt his jaw drop. The brain scan highlighted over-stimulated areas within Darrin's brain. The most activity occurred in the frontal lobe. The other data showed increased neuro-activity spiking off the charts. Both men stood, trying to make sense of what they were looking at.

"What have I done?" John muttered covering his mouth with his hands.

"John, we've got to finish this, tell him to open is eyes. I want to see how the optical signals from his eyes affect his brain wave patterns."

"What are you thinking?"

"I think the M1-28 might have unintentionally unlocked dormant sections of his consciousness that humans don't normally use. Whatever the M1 did for his vision, it also did for his higher brain functions," he said leaning closer to John, "finish it."

The knot tightened in his stomach. His desire to help his son blinded him to any consequences. Before he decided to use the M1 on Darrin, he poured over the animal trial results for weeks and found nothing that foresaw what appeared on the screen.

"Darrin, son, I know you're scared, but I need you to open your eyes."

"Dad?" Darrin's voice quivered on the edge of tears.

"Please, only for a few moments and then we'll have all the data we'll need to work with."

Darrin inhaled deeply and did the one thing he'd feared all day, he opened his eyes wide.

***

The lab windows began rattling and the lights dimmed and brightened. The scanner's instruments hummed loudly and the glass screens exploded. The room's lights glowed like a sun popped out as if they were gunshots. The men felt the floor shake and the building quaked. With one last push, the lights went out leaving them in total darkness.

"Everyone stay put! The emergency lights will kick on in a moment. Tony, I want you to get Darrin when we can see again," hollered Edward.

John could hear the whimpers from his son.

"I'm going to get him. I've got the screen light from my phone to help me find my way," Tony yelled out.

"Be careful," John answered and stood to see Tony move slowly through the room.

When Tony neared the scanner his phone died out and then in the pitch black he screamed. His agonizing shriek ceased when the emergency lights came on and lit up the room. The dim lights shone on Tony's body floating six feet above the floor. John looked at the tile beneath Tony's feet and watched as his head rolled toward the control room glass. Blood poured from the torn flesh around his neck and flowed like a river down his chest to the floor.

John and Edward stared in horror. Another ripping sound filled the air and both Tony's arms flew and smacked on the window in front of them splashing gore and chunks of meat on the glass. The bits slid down leaving slimy crimson trails of sinew and blood behind.

John shook off the shock and yelled at Darrin, "Shut them now! Shut your eyes!"

He could barely make out Darrin's shape in the scanner, but he saw movement. In front of his eyes, Tony's floating body folded in on its self and cracked while his flesh and bones crushed like a wadded piece of paper until his remains vanished into nothing.

John frantically kicked the chairs from in front of the glass windows and began pounding his fist on them.

***

Darrin gazed out into the spot and watched the grayish-green appendages emerge from the spot and reach out into the world. He thought he heard his father yelling at him, but he

121

couldn't make the words out. All he heard was the steady calling of the spot.

"*Sleeper, Sleeper, Sleeper,*" it repeated over and over.

Realizing he had to stop it, he tried to close his eyes. His eyelids held firm, the thrashing tentacles preventing him from closing them. Rotating his wrists around, he found the bindings were loose and began trying to slip his arms free. Wiggling his thin wrists, he pulled free of the restraints. Sitting up, he looked at the control room and saw his father slamming his fists into the glass.

Quickly, he wormed his way out of the scanner and looked around. The black hole in his vision consumed almost all of his sight, leaving him nearly blind again. On the periphery, he glimpsed his father and Edward both beating on the glass mouthing something to him. He focused, trying to make out their words, but they were muffled by the thick safety glass and the noise in his head.

The tentacles battered everything in their path reducing the examination equipment into twist, smoking hunks of metal. They tore through everything and the building began to shake violently again. The emergency lights flickered and Darrin covered his eyes with his hands. He heard the strange limbs still destroying the lab and ripping into the ceiling. Pointless, he dropped his hands down and started lumbering toward the control room.

***

John and Edward stood in shock. Something crashed through the lab, but they didn't see anything except the dents magically appear in the machines and the fixtures ripped free of the floor by an invisible force. A loud thumping sounded out and cracks spread throughout the thick glass. Looking out through the white and blue sparks arcing through the room, they saw Darrin slowly approach them.

Another loud crash filled the room and parts of the glass gave out and fell, slamming into the floor.

"John, you have to get him to stop!" Edward shouted over the banging in the room.

"I don't think he can Edward! Whatever it is, he can't control it!" John screamed back.

The glass burst like a dam and the men were showered in glass. Shards flew and pierced their arms and faces, slicing them to the bone. They cried out from the cuts digging in their flesh.

Edward got to his feet and ran toward the door, but he felt something grab his ankle. Looking down, he didn't see anything and tugged on his leg. His leg yanked out from beneath him and he crashed to the floor. His breath escaped him and laid there panting, trying to get air to his lungs for one last escape chance. Rolling onto his stomach, Edward began crawling to the door. The quaking caused the door to fall over, but any way to freedom worked so he moved forward. A swift tug halted him and he felt the thing around his ankle constrict. Before he could try again he felt himself flung off the floor and hovering in the air.

John quietly reached out for Edward when he began to slam onto the hard tile floor again and again. The first few times he heard the crunching of bones and by the time he'd counted to ten, it sounded like a ball of ground beef being thrown against a brick wall. Trying to be quiet, John retreated back under the desk while Edward disappeared into nothingness.

Darrin stepped through the broken glass and looked down at his father. Trying to close his eyes one last time, he could stop the tentacles from latching on to his father and devouring him into the void.

Then Darrin had an idea.

***

Olivia rushed in the front door expecting to see her husband and son excited to see her back. Instead she found the house empty and a note taped to the mirror next to the door. Hope swelled in her heart as she finished the note. Quickly, she picked her keys and purse back up and ran to the car.

Her trip to the James Pharmaceuticals complex sped by. In her rear view, sirens wailed and she pulled over to let them pass. Above her, she heard the whirring of helicopters and wondered what the emergency was. Her foot pressed down harder on the accelerator. A sense of dread filled her the closer she came to the complex. The flashing blue and red lights illuminated the night sky in the direction of her husband's lab. Speeding up faster, Olivia shot off down the road to her family.

Her fear was justified. Pulling to the guard shack, she could see all the police, sheriffs, and ambulances in front of the crumbling building. The right wing of the building had collapsed and the sparking electricity lit up the night. News helicopters circled the area flooding the ground with spotlights.

A cop stopped her when she pulled toward the parking lot.

"Excuse me miss, this is an emergency situation and I'm going to have to ask you to leave please."

"But my husband, my son," she started before she burst into tears.

"How old is your son?"

"He's ten and his name is Darrin," she answered between sniffles.

"Please, come with me now," he said and started speaking into his radio.

Olivia climbed from the Volvo and the officer quickly led her through the commotion to an ambulance off to the right. The rear doors were open and a paramedic worked on someone sitting on the back bumper. She rounded the corner, looked beyond the doors, and screamed.

Darrin sat on the back with bandages wrapped around his head and padding covering his eyes. Streaks of blood still ran down his cheeks and stained his collar.

"Oh my God, Darrin," Olivia cried out and rushed to embrace her son.

"Are you his mother?" the paramedic asked.

"Yes, yes I am," she said stroking her son's hair. "What happened?"

"He has lost the use of his eyes and…"

"My son was blind," she mumbled.

"Mommy? I could see, Daddy helped me see again," whispered Darrin.

"What happened baby?"

"I could see, but I saw something else too and it did this. I stopped it, I stopped it mommy. I saved everyone in the building except daddy, Uncle Edward, and Mr. Tony."

Olivia placed her fingers underneath the bandage and lifted. She stifled back a scream when she saw her son's eyes were scratched out and his eyeballs were reduced to bloody chunks in his eye sockets. Blood tears still trailed down his cheeks.

"I had to close the gate; I put the Sleeper back in the void and the voices stopped."

Olivia hugged her son harder and wept while the search went on for her husband and the dawn approached from the east.

***

STORY NOTES:

This is one I consider one of my best pieces and one I am very proud of. There are a lot of things running through here. First, it is a loosely-tied White Creek story. It doesn't have anything to do with the direct mythos, but the company and Darrin will be back again in the future. Second, is that this is my love letter to H.P. Lovecraft. I treaded very lightly around his mythos, but I hope the feel and scope of the story fit in. Thirdly, I was in a phase exploring fathers and sons and the basis of how Darrin regains his sight came from that. Overall, the story was difficult to write however. I rewrote the first half almost five times as I tried to find the right feel for Darrin when he first begins to see again. In the end, I love the image of Olivia rushing to her son's aid and seeing the price he paid for sealing the rift. Remember, it's all about sacrifice…

FOR OUR SINS: A FABLE

1

"Do you think the wolf can see us?" the priestess said to her handmaiden.

"My lady, why do you spy on the wolf so? For three nights you sit here on the balcony and follow every move it makes."

"Look at him, watch the way the muscles move beneath the fur, and how his eyes shine in the moonlight," the priestess said as her wanting burned her down to her core.

The handmaiden squinted into the night to observe the wolf better. She turned to the priestess, "My dear Katharine, I see not what you see in that mongrel beast!"

"Do you know how hard it is that I can never know the touch of another? To not feel anything so I can remain pure and virginal? I only wish to feel the loving touch of another."

"Are you not pure of the mind?"

Katharine giggled, "Oh no, my Danni, my mind is not pure!"

"Well I'm going to bed, you better hope the High Priest doesn't find out what thoughts go through your head," Danni said. She exited the room and pulled the door shut behind her.

Katharine listened for Danni's footfalls to fade off down the hallway. When they ended she untied her robe and let it fall to the floor. Stepping out of it, she perched back on the balcony, her alabaster flesh naked in the moonbeams. In the moonlight filtering through the treetops, she could see the silver refractions of his eyes. She gently caressed her fingers over her body and a small moan escaped her lips. She prayed in her mind that the high priest didn't barge in. Her situation would be seen as unfortunate and the punishment scared her. Caught in the moment, she allowed her fingers to roam across her soft skin and gently touch the places burning her and melting her interior even in the evening's chill. She felt like her soul was aflame as she drove herself to madness while her eyes stayed fixed on the wolf at the edge of the woods.

***

Out in the night the wolf paced around the forest's edge, watching the tower where soft candle light silhouetted a figure on the balcony. He hungered and the knot deep in his gut kept bringing him to the edge of his pack's hunting grounds looking for food. The local villagers decimated the deer, rabbits, and squirrels leaving him, the alpha, unable to provide for the pack. Gazing back up at the human, he felt the rush in his belly like at the start of a hunt. Alas, it was impossible to hunt humans. The wolf god, Hemming, forbade the wolves from hunting and consuming the man-flesh. His stomach grumbled again. The alpha raised his head to the full moon and howled a prayer to Hemming.

***

Hemming sat in the heavens and heard the troubled cry of his beloved alpha wolf. He paced the clouds and like his wolves, he too grew tired of the blood oath between him and the earth goddess Demeter. The pact kept the humans from being feasted upon by the wolves. The virgin sacrifice every four years to Hemming grew increasingly less and less fulfilling to him. Hemming, like his wolves, wanted to taste man-flesh again. He hadn't partaken of a human in over four hundred and twelve years. He looked back down at the alpha that invoked him and noticed he paced on the outskirts of Demeter's temple complex.

When he heard the silent longings from the priestess cross his ears, he smiled. Thinking for a moment, he found his way to break the oath.

***

Katharine sat on the balcony floor panting and sweating. She watched the wolf trot back into the forest and she sighed, her heart hammering in her chest from her explorations. Her trembling hands gripped the ledge and she pulled herself up and bending over, snatched her robe from the floor. The cool silk felt good on her sweat slickened skin. Katharine began to tie her robe when someone cleared their throat behind her.

A man dressed in peasant garb stood on the balcony where she stood only a few moments before. He looked caked in dirt and stank like the waste pit behind the temple. A wolf pelt covered his shoulders.

"Who are you and how did you get in here?" Katharine uttered in surprise.

"I only want to answer your prayers, the ones your so-called goddess refuses to grant you an answer to."

"Answer me true or I shall summon the guards."

Hemming stroked his chin and smiled, exposing the tips of his fangs. "I can give you what you desire."

"How do you know what I desire?"

"The cries from your soul reached me, so I brought you a gift," he said, removing the pelt from his shoulders. "This can give you your heart's desire, the love you yearn for."

"What will a wolf pelt do for love?" She asked reaching out for it.

"On the next full moon, when the silver wolf appears, go to the temple gardens and place the pelt on your naked body. The pelt will then grant you your desires."

"How do you know what my heart desires? You appear in my chambers and presume to know what I want?"

He turned with a grin, "Oh my dear vestal virgin, the gods can hear all. I have heard your call and I am here to help you."

Katharine took the pelt from his outstretched hands and rubbed the fur against her soft cheek. She wrapped the pelt around her shoulders and pulled it in tight around her body to ward off the cool breeze blowing in from the open windows. Turning back around to thank the man, she found him no longer standing in her room, but on the balcony. He winked at her and jumped off into the night. Rushing over, she screamed and found nothing on the ground where he would have landed, but she swore she could still hear him laughing.

Thunderous footsteps echoed in the hall outside her room. Katharine quickly pulled her robe on and kicked the pelt under her bed as the door came crashing in and three guards rushed in.

"What is going on? Are you alright?" asked the High Priest, pushing through the guards blocking the door.

"Nothing, Iden, I thought I heard something on the balcony and I found only a big spider."

"You must be careful; in three lunar cycles you will perform the ritual that is your birthright. We must have you chaste and pure to ensure the ritual works. Many lives depend on you Katharine." He turned to the guards and waved them off. "I will keep an extra eye on you for these last cycles I fear. I sense something afoot and the earth mother is not happy. You will go to the temple now and supplicate yourself to her alter."

Iden turned curtly around and stormed out of room leaving Katharine to prepare herself for supplication. The lashes would leave their marks, but while putting on her prayer robes she glanced down at the pelt and smiled. The lunar cycle for the priestess would be a long one.

***

Outside the window, Hemming morphed into wolf form and ran up into the heavens.

***

On the forest's edge, the alpha noticed this and slinked back into the woods hoping this meant food.

***

High priest Iden felt Hemming's presence and watched as the wolf departed back into the night sky. Something was happening and it didn't please him at all.

***

Meanwhile, in the temple, Katharine accepted her lashings at the altar with a look of contentment on her face.

2

The lunar cycle did prove to be long and daunting for the priestess. The days crept by and the nights brought time to a halt while Katharine longed for the full moon's return. She slept with the wolf pelt as a blanket and told no one, not even Danni, of her encounter one month ago.

Danni left for the night and Katharine immediately hopped out of bed and ran to the balcony. The full moon broke through the last of the cloud cover and illuminated the temple grounds below. Quickly, she threw off her robe and started to feel the burn in her loins while she felt slickness between her legs. Her breath quickened, her fingers explored her figure, and then she saw the wolf appear on the grounds.

Katharine wasted no time grabbing the pelt and rushing to the secret chamber door behind her devotional altar. She silently stalked down the passageway leading to the gardens. In the middle where there stood a statue of Demeter, the wolf would meet her, she remembered the man saying. The dreams that had faded away with the waning of the last full moon came rushing back with the appearance of the full moon.

The gardens were situated in a large circular shape with two entrances on the outer ring of bushes and the path spiraled along a shorter and shorter route until it ended at Demeter's alter in the center. The shrine contained her totem, areas to pray, and devices for supplication to the goddess. Katharine hurried through the rings, listening for her love. She reached the shrine and saw her wolf pacing along the altar.

Up close she found him breathtaking. Something within her stirred and giving in to her lust, she took the pelt and draped it around her naked body. Suddenly it latched into her flesh and she felt the heat between her thighs rise to an unbearable needing. Her legs gave out from underneath her and falling to the ground, she landed on four legs with a coat of fur.

The pelt granted her the power of the wolf.

The alpha drew back in alarm. What was once human, now sat before him as a mate. He detected the twang of her fertility in the air and cautiously approached. Her new ears perked up at the sound of his paws behind her. She heard him back away, but then he mounted her and his claws dug into her back. For a split second, she felt pressure in her hindquarters and a touch of pain as the alpha gave into his animalistic nature.

Within a few seconds the act ended and the alpha climbed down from her. He turned back towards the woods and ran into the darkness leaving her empty and unfulfilled. A low growl emanated from her in anger. Every prayer, every oath, every moment and breath of her life were now shattered in her moment of weakness.

***

In the shrine, next to Demeter's statue, Hemming laughed knowing the pact was now voided.

***

Katharine lay on the ground and the pelt slipped from her shoulders. Without the pelt, she reverted smoothly back to her own human body. She rolled over, hearing the footfalls behind her. Hemming strolled over and patted her on the head like she was still a wolf. He bent over, picked the pelt up, and threw it over his shoulder.

"Thank you my child. We have suffered over four hundred years of hunger under your goddess. I was patient and I waited. Now because of your transgressions, the truce between Demeter and myself is over. Now we shall ravage the countryside and feast on the flesh of men again!"

A loud thunder crack shook the shrine as the high priest slammed his staff down onto the garden's floor. He muttered a few quick words and Hemming found he couldn't move. Iden moved towards Hemming and got eye to eye with him.

"What have you done?" he screamed at Hemming.

"I have done what my children bade me to do, undo the covenant between man and wolf. We will now take our rightful place in nature!" Hemming stated as he licked the tips of his fangs in the high priest's face.

Iden glared at Katharine. "Go and cloth yourself. Punishment for your part in this matter will be severe on both fronts," he ordered her in disgust.

Hemming tried to move and found his feet unable to step away; he remained grounded where he stood. He disrobed and wrapping the pelt around him tried to morph, but he stayed in his human form.

"How do you trap a god?" Hemming asked and his fury with the high priest evident in his tone.

"My devotion to my goddess has been rewarded. Now the power to punish you for your deeds also falls to me. You will lead me to the pack, the alpha and his kin must suffer."

The high priest reached over and felt Katharine's stomach. Through the insight the goddess granted him, he felt the stirrings of a new life already stirring within her womb. He sighed and dropped his hand back to his side. Deep down he always knew the girl had failure's taint. The first day she came to the temple, the portents were bad and the omens unfavorable. His doubt was overridden by the will of the goddess and like a sheep, he followed her wishes.

Now everything that stood for four hundred years came crashing down on his watch and he would make those responsible pay. The high priest stood with his head bowed and prayed for the goddess's intervention. He needed her strength and grace to do what he found himself tasked to do.

"Hemming, you will take me to the pack, now," ordered the high priest, turning towards the forest.

Hemming laughed and stood his ground. "You can't force me to do anything Iden; you are a mere mortal with no authority over us gods."

High priest Iden turned back to Hemming and tapped his staff on the ground three times. Hemming cried out in pain and dropped to his knees. He looked up at Iden and spat on his feet. The priest slowly raised his hand and Hemming rose from the ground to his feet.

"You will follow me. Katharine, you will join us into the forest. Your actions are an affront to our religion and to the will of the goddess. Your lust and selfishness has ended the peace between us and the wolves. The gates have been thrown open for them to rampage through the countryside eating and devouring all in their path." He turned from Katharine to Hemming, "and you engineered this. I shall let you bear witness to the punishment Demeter is handing down to your precious pack."

Iden walked into the forest while Katharine and Hemming followed. Katharine's head stared at the ground in shame and humiliation while Hemming walked next to her with a mask of rage and anger. He seethed at being pushed around and controlled by a human. He struggled to walk a different path, but his body remained bound to the path Iden walked.

3

Elsewhere in the moonlit forest, the alpha returned to the pack. His arrival back meant food the other wolves thought, but instead he came trotting back with nothing and they smelled the stink of human on him. His mate got up from their young and came sniffing around him. She smelled the fertility blood tainting him and growled. Another large wolf came over and joined her in her angry barks. Soon the entire pack circled him, howling their disapproval.

"Enough!" shouted a human form walking into their lair.

The wolves turned and barked at him. Not only was the alpha stricken, but he also brought humans to them. Two other forms entered and stood behind the robed man with the staff. The shape in the back with the pelt on his shoulder waved his hand and the wolves sat down silently on their haunches and watched. The other human shared the seasoned stink their alpha had on him.

"Your alpha has committed the gravest of all sins and for that the pack must pay the penalty."

Iden tapped his staff on the ground as the pack began pacing in front of him, ready to pounce. The alpha quickly dropped to the ground yelping and howling out in agony for his god to save him. Hemming reached out to him and Iden motioned for him to drop his outstretched hand. The alpha bayed at the full moon that now was forsaking him.

His skin began to tingle and his silver coat started to recede from his body. A loud snapping followed as his paws began to expand and grow out. The claws that once protected and provided for the pack pulled back into his half-formed fingers leaving a bloody path in their wake. The tendons and muscles slid and shifted, separated and formed new configurations. His jaw dislocated with a sickening crack and shortened back towards his face, his fangs retreating into his gum line. His tail folded back and grew into the base of his spine.

The transformation went on slowly for untold minutes while Iden watched, Katharine wept, and Hemming turned his head away so he didn't have to witness the scene before him. When the change ended, a naked man laid on the forest floor before them. Without his thick coat, he shivered in the cool autumn breeze. His once silver eyes gazed up at Hemming with a new brown hue and a look of betrayal. Iden, Hemming, and Katharine backed away from the scene as the pack began to circle their changed leader.

His mate approached him and sniffed the sick stench of his new body making the hair on her back raise. She growled at him and he could see the anger, hunger, and hurt flaming through her amber eyes. He reached out to her to comfort her and she snapped her jaws at his quickly retreating fingers. The other members joined her in her growling.

Iden walked over and stood next to the alpha. He struck his staff into the ground again and muttered an ancient rite. Howls of pain erupted from the pack, their own transformations beginning. Writhing on the ground, each one changed into human form and not even the pups were spared.

Katharine rushed over to Iden and pleaded, "Stop this! They're innocent."

"My child, none are innocent in this matter. They are receiving their due and you will now get yours. You are hereby exiled to live the rest of your life with them. Your child can be raised by its mother and father out here in the wilderness. You will teach them and integrate them into the world of man."

"Our child?"

"Oh, yes, I can already sense it growing within you. My work here is finished, I shall return to the temple and meditate on our goddess's new intentions," he said. Without speaking, he turned and walked off into the night.

Katharine rushed to the alpha's side and brushed his hair from his new beautiful human face. She looked around at the rest of the pack and sighed, her prison for the rest of her life. A tear fell down her cheek.

Hemming bent down and whispered in her ear, "I still have some say in this my lady. I can't undo what has been done, but I can grant a small reprieve."

The wolf god stood back up and began whispering to the full moon. Katharine got up and came over to him.

"What did you do?"

"I have given my wolves a gift. On the full moon, those humans who descend from this pack's bloodline will be granted the power to return to their native form when the moon shines full and bright. For those days, they can be wolves until the moon begins to wane again. I wish I could grant them more, but I am limited in what my power as a lesser deity can do."

"Thank you," whispered Katharine as she lowered her head and returned to the human pack.

Hemming shifted into a wolf and ran off into the approaching dawn.

4

"That is some story," the psychologist said, putting her pen down on her desk.

"Look Dr. Shelby, it's true. My grandmother told me the story when I turned ten, to... you know, explain certain changes in my body."

"So, your family can change into wolves on the full moon? I think you need further evaluation, because it sounded more like you found hair in new places," she taunted and rolled her tongue across the top of her pen.

"You have no idea honey," the man said sitting upright on the couch

Dr. Shelby picked her pen back up and began writing. Jonathan stood up and paced the room, his eyes darting to the window every few seconds. The moon remained hidden behind the blanket of clouds. He felt his rising agitation and broke out into a sweat, drenching his tee shirt.

"Beth, look I just want to clear things up between us."

"Hey, you're the one who decided it was a good idea to ask me out months ago."

"You have to know that story from my grandmother wasn't a euphemism for puberty. She was telling the origins of my kind and about my curse."

"I guess you were bitten or something?"

"Beth! You have to listen; my curse doesn't transfer through a bite. It is transferred through my bloodline, only my family can change back and forth between man and wolf. My family's name 'Whalen' is Celtic for wolf."

"Why are you telling me this shit now? Ha, ha, very funny, do you want me to leave and this is your way of forcing me to end it, with some story about you being a werewolf? Jesus Jonathan, I love you and right now you need help! Let me help you," Beth pleaded on the verge of tears.

In the sky the moon rays started to sneak out from behind the clouds. They danced on the floor in front of Jonathan's feet. He felt the heat rise within him like his blood was boiling. He shook violently and fell to the floor.

"Oh my god, are you ok Jonathan?"

"You will… be… protected. You carry our child. I can't hurt… you," he grunted and rolled over.

"Our child?"

"Have… to… show," he screamed in agony and looked up at Beth, his eyes an amber hue.

"No, no, no," she repeated over and over while she watched her lover sprout coarse silver fur from his pores and claws in front of her. Jonathan let out an ear splitting howl towards the window and ripped his tee shirt and jeans to shreds.

Then she felt something in her stomach move.

**

STORY NOTES:

"For Our Sins: A Fable" is one of my first sales and is the one story my mother finally told me she liked. I don't think I ever set out to do the werewolf/zombie/vampire thing, but it just happened. It's hard to turn away from the traditional monsters that influenced you as a kid. For this story I wanted to give the werewolf an origin story, a 'where did they come from?' tale. When I came up with the premise, I did some research into Celtic names and meanings. This is the reason people and beasts are named what they are throughout the story. Overall, the story was fun to write and it had the honor of closing out the anthology it appeared in.

THE MIDNIGHT RIDER

Greg slammed on the brakes, squealing the tires and almost careened the hearse off the guardrail. The black Mustang had appeared out of nowhere and swerved in front of Greg, missing him by mere inches. Driving for your family's funeral home was one thing, but hauling your mother's corpse to her hometown was something else entirely, and the jackass in front of him only made the situation worse.

Greg regained control of the hearse and floored the gas pedal, his ire provoked. The Mustang's brake lights flashed ahead so he let off the gas a little. He was pissed they cut him off, but now the fact they were going to play games on the moonlit highway really got his blood boiling. He crept up to the Mustang's bumper and braked so he could tailgate. Through the dark night, moonlight shone through the treetops and illuminated a sticker on the tinted back window.

Greg squinted to read it and giggled as he read it aloud.

"*Please Don't Hit ME!* I can't believe it... Really?" He slammed his hands on the steering wheel.

The highway grew darker as the clouds covered the moon. The pavement stretched out before them as he stayed right on the Mustang's tail. Sixty miles ahead, he would deliver his cargo and then drive the hearse back for the Marshall funeral in the morning. The Mustang slowly started to accelerate, so Greg matched it.

Suddenly, the brake lights flashed and Greg braked hard to keep the hearse from hitting the Mustang's rear bumper. Glancing at the sticker again, he noticed something odd. It had changed.

Did You Cook the Books Again? She Knows!

"What the fuck?"

Thirty years old and he still lived at home with his parents behind the funeral home. He wasn't the greatest looking guy and he'd never really hit it off with the ladies, but he was good with numbers and things of the sort. Greg's primary job at the funeral home was to take care of the accounting. Once he delved into the myriad world of ledgers, numbers, and statements, he'd found making slight alterations was easy. Within a year, he milked the business out of ten thousand dollars. Everything was going smoothly until he left an altered ledger page on his desk. His mother found it while looking for the stapler and confronted him.

The family ate dinner together in silence for two weeks. The strict Christian household brought other punishments as well. He thought she'd gone overboard considering he was twenty-eight at the time, but his parents made him pray for hours that Jesus would cleanse his soiled soul. His father locked the door to the chapel in the funeral home, leaving Greg with his thoughts, a bible, and a picture of Christ for conversation. He ended up talking to himself and sleeping for days at a time. Greg found he really was his own best friend, carrying on many deep conversations with himself. He found nobody else mattered except the version of himself he spoke to for hours on end about life and how he hated his. Sometimes, he felt a seething hate pulse within his body so strongly, he didn't think he'd be able to draw it back into himself.

His mind focused back to the window's sticker and its ability to see he was embezzling money again. What bothered Greg was how did it know? Even more troubling was the changing sticker. He knew what it said before he'd caught back up and it was not what he just read.

The brake lights slammed on again in front of him and Greg turned the wheel to the left. The hearse skidded as he avoided the Mustang. Flying into the other lane, he over-corrected sending the hearse close to the embankment on the side of the country highway. Swinging the hearse's tail-end back around, he straightened out it out and got back behind the Mustang. Greg knew he wanted to talk to the driver... *Now*! He wanted to know how they did the sticker trick and how they knew his private secrets.

Before his eyes, the words melted and rearranged themselves into something new.

Did You Plan It? Did She Know?

The Mustang pulled away from Greg and sped off down the highway. He stomped down on the pedal to keep pace with the Mustang.

They knew.

Somehow, they knew what happened and Greg wondered if they saw him when he went about his work that night; delicate work only a loving son could do. He brought his mother a rose from the garden with dinner and read her the newspaper like he did every night while his father prepared the bodies for showings or funerals the next day. He lovingly fed her spoonfuls of vegetable soup and carefully wiped her chin clean with a napkin. Greg was such a loving son. He gently tilted the glass of ice-cold lemonade to her lips, letting her take small sips.

After she'd finished her last meal, he went about his task. Taking her favorite pillow he gently placed it over her face and smothered his mother's cancer ridden body. She tried to fight, thrashing about, but his weight pushed her down into the mattress as he struggled with what little strength she had left. Greg held the pillow in place until he felt her body's last feeble attempt to break free. Her weakened body gave out after a few minutes. Listening to her last gasping breath beneath the pillow, he shed a tear as he pulled it away. Greg found himself gazing into her accusatory dead eyes. Gathering his emotions, he closed her eyes for the final time and finished the deed of preparing the room for the discovery of her freshly dead corpse.

He thought he used the utmost care. He planned it all out in his mind during the hours he spent 'praying for forgiveness' in the chapel. Greg executed it flawlessly and even had the room ready so when his father came upstairs from the parlor, it looked like she'd died in her sleep.

But now the perfect crime looked less than perfect.

Someone knew.

Obviously he'd been wrong; someone had seen him that night and they were right in front of him, flaunting the fact they knew. Teasing him and taunting him as they drove on ahead. He pressed on, closing the gap while the engine bucked and howled in protest.

The speedometer on the hearse's dash reached ninety miles per hour. If the Mustang accelerated much faster, Greg knew he would lose it and the other driver. In the opposite lane, another set of headlights filled his vision. The Mustang switched lanes and began racing head-on toward the other vehicle in a game of chicken. Greg never imagined he'd be racing the hearse while on the clock when he decided to work in the family business. His time to catch a glimpse of the other driver was passing. Soon they'd hit the Miller Creek bridge and he'd lose them. Common sense dictated he stay away from there. He'd heard the stories about what goes on there and didn't feel like becoming one of the tales spun around local campfires.

He coaxed a little more speed out of the hearse, pushing the pedal deeper into the floor. If he tried to depress the gas pedal harder, he'd put his foot through the floorboard. He caught up to the side of the Mustang in only a few moments. The headlights in the other lane continued to grow larger and larger. The Mustang never wavered, speeding toward the other vehicle. Greg pulled up and peeked over into the other car. The windows were so darkly tinted, he couldn't make out anything inside. The Mustang drifted closer to the side of the hearse, and Greg moved over to the outside of his lane, not letting the Mustang come all the way over.

The Mustang driver didn't appear to panic, even as the headlights neared to a few hundred feet. Suddenly, the Mustang's speed exploded, cutting him off again as it entered the lane in front of him. The passing semi honked his horn and flashed his highbeams as it blew by, disappearing into the night.

Greg braked hard again, slowing before he rammed the Mustang.

I Know What You're Thinking.

He pounded his fists on the steering wheel harder and shouted, "Who the hell are you! I was alone!"

The two cars sped through the night with Miller Creek and the town of White Creek dead ahead. He had ten minutes left to end this chase. He gripped the wheel so tight his knuckles turned white and his hand felt like needles pricked his flesh. The speedometer's needle nudged up to 97. The engine started to rattle, pushed to its limits.

The Mustang braked and fishtailed to the right, spinning off onto another road. Its tires spun in the gravel and took off again. Greg slammed down on the brakes and they barked in disagreement. The brakes locked and he jerked the wheel to the right so he wouldn't pass the old farm access road. He took his foot off the brake and jammed it back down on the gas. The hearse sputtered in protest, but then the engine roared back to life. The coffin in the back slid forward when the hearse peeled out over the gravel and accelerated in pursuit of the Mustang.

Greg's breathing became fast and sweat beaded on his forehead. The pistons under the hood were driving as hard as his heart pounded in his chest. Up ahead, he watched the Mustang stop. It turned around and Greg found it pointing right at him, its headlights staring at him like a pair of judging eyes.

In the distance he heard the engine rev and squeal out as it shot toward the hearse. Without thinking, Greg went faster. Fury coursed through his veins, seething anger controlling him now. He tried searching his head for the other him he talked to. Greg held out hope he could talk himself out of his current course of action. Nobody answered.

His mother's corpse banged around the back in protest. The metal sliding on metal made groaning sounds and he wondered if she was mad at him for taking her corpse on a wild ride. Greg looked back at his mother and checked his seatbelt, making sure it was tight.

"I'm sorry mom, but I can't let them turn me in."

The distance closed between them. The Mustang's lights turned off, leaving it visible only in the silver moonlight. Greg flashed his and then turned them off altogether. His body stiffened up, bracing for the impact.

"I'll show you damn it! I'll see you in hell!"

The two cars hit head on. Greg threw his arms up in front of his face to protect it from flying glass, but Greg realized something wasn't right- he didn't feel the impact. When he looked around, the Mustang sat beside him with the window down.

Greg looked across and found himself staring back, his spectral twin mouthing the word "murderer". The reflection of Greg driving the Mustang winked and threw a rose on the hearse's top before fading away into the night. Confused, Greg turned back toward the road in time to see the tree cut through the hearse's hood and the steering wheel crush his chest. He panted, his breath becoming labored like something covered his face, smothering him and his sins.

Darkness crept into his vision and he noticed a bright spot of color in his peripheral. The crimson rose floated down through the window and landed on Greg's lap as he took his last breath.

The funeral home sticker in the back window swam around. One by one, the lines and curves slid around the glass and reformed.

The sticker read…

Justice.

***

STORY NOTES:

"Midnight Rider" was written for a charity anthology based on drive-in movies. Most of the book centered on monsters and creatures, so I decided to take a different route. Growing up, I loved those old Seventies race and chase movies. I wanted to see cars go fast and crash hard. I also have a love of the Ford Mustang and wanted to write a short little ghostly revenge story based around a car chase. The other thing I wanted to explore was how guilt can either make you see and do weird stuff or how your guilt can summon something else to pay out the justice you have coming.

THOSE LAST MINUTES

I know I look ridiculous right now. I'm sure the people around me are snickering and cracking a quick joke at the weird guy sitting alone on the park bench with his mouth hanging wide open. Well shit, how would they feel if they just found out their lives would more or less end in an hour and a half. Really though, after everything I've been through in my thirty-seven years on this planet, and it all ends in ninety minutes.

I never should have trusted Dirty Johnny. That old booze-hound came sniffing around the park like he usually does, looking for some loose change, or hoping somebody dropped a potato chip on the ground. I've seen that dirty, old bum scare off the birds just so he could eat the bread crumbs an old lady tossed to the ground. Three hours ago, I only thought he wanted change for a coffee or a bagel.

Nope, of course not... he wanted a bite of me.

I knew I was in deep shit once I took a good look at the film covering his eyes as his rotted and crooked teeth sank into my ankle. All I wanted to do was my good deed for the day, but no, I got screwed in the end. That's the world we live in today, one where the living have to cover their asses on the city streets to keep from becoming undead meat. If you're lucky, they'll eat you. If you're not so lucky, like me, they bite and loose interest. They'll up and leave you to wait it out while the virus courses through your system until you join the zombie brotherhood.

But anyway, I kicked him in the face to drive him off, and rushed across the street to the drug store to pick me up a bite kit. Dealing with the zombies in our society sucks, but the people who made pregnancy tests figured out how to alter a blood-glucose meter into a device that tells someone who's bitten how long until they go all undead on everyone around. And once you know the countdown, all bets are off.

How they figured out a way to predict how long you have, is beyond me, but I know they work. I've seen them in action. I remember the day my friend Louis got bit at the bowling alley on league night. He ran straight to the store and bought a test. Quit the game mid-frame. Once he read how long he had left, he went on a cocaine, booze, and whore bender like the world had never seen.

I hated killing him two hours later, but he died happy. At least I think he did…

Great, now I'm down to eighty-one minutes. I'm not much of a drug-and-hooker type of guy, so now what? Well, I always wanted to tell some people what I really thought about them. Ya know, since my brain will pretty much be a clean, albeit empty slate, I should go and begin my goodbyes.

Who should I go to first? My mom and dad? No, deep down I think I should wait until after I change to go and see them. Heather? Yeah, I'll go say goodbye to her first. I'd hate for her to come home wanting some quality time, and the only thing I want is rip her head apart and slurp on her brains. God, she is the only thing that's gone right for me these past few years.

WICKED TALES FOR WICKED PEOPLE

Should I take her something? Like, I don't know, a small trinket that says, 'I love you', or 'I hope I don't eat your brains today'. The greeting card companies haven't quite caught on to this particular dilemma, which really surprises me since they made cards for 'Boss's Day'. Who the hell likes their boss that much anyway? Maybe some flowers and a box of chocolates will smooth things over.

Seventy-five minutes left. Damn, I feel hot. My veins are on fire, and I can feel the virus spread rapidly through my body. I walk into the flower shop, and my arms itch uncontrollably. In the middle of ordering, I slowly scratch my arm. While the clerk gathers and wraps the pink roses I picked out, my fingernails dig deeper and deeper into my skin, trying to sooth the burning under the top layers of my flesh. I force a smile when he drops the bouquet on the counter, and covers his mouth in horror. Honestly, I think the man is being quite rude until I look down, and see the beads of blood dripping from my arm.

"Take the flowers, they're free," he yells at me, and signs the cross on his chest. When I reach to grab the flowers, he jumps back, and his eyes are so wide, I swear they are going to bug out of his head. For good measure I reach across the counter, grab a box of dark chocolate, and whisper to the old man.

"Boo!" I gave him a heart-attack.

Upon exiting the store, I stop in the middle of the sidewalk, and take a deep breath of the sour city air. Funny, I never noticed how bad the smell really is until now. I wonder if it's the virus kicking in, or if I've just ignored it as I passed through my usual daily routine. How much have I missed out on in life?

My shoulder jerks violently, and the flowers fall from my hands. I'm stunned for a moment, and I can only watch as the roses land on the ground and some of the lovely petals fall from the thorny stems. Nice allegory for my life right now…

The tremor subsides, and I bend over to pick the flowers up, and notice my joints feel stiff. I can feel the coordination leaving my limbs. My fingers try to grasp the flowers, and finally on the eighth try, I snatch them from the pavement and slowly rise back up.

Sixty-nine minutes.

Why is it time flies when you wish it would slow down? I walk to the apartment, and man my legs feel like lead. I was hoping to make it further before it hit me this hard. Oh my God, it got real hot fast. Well, not the weather, but last time I felt this feverish, I ran a temp of one o' four.

Damn, people are staring. Three blocks down, and fifty minutes to go. Did I seriously just hear my name? I look around, and at first I don't hear anyone until I see that six-foot-six motherfucker hollering at me and running my way.

"Jeff! Hey Jeff! Wait up, man!" His deep voice calls out.

Oh, man, I don't have time for his shit. I walk on like I never heard him, but I messed up when I turned my head the first time I heard his voice. I swear I can't win. Not even on the day I get bit by a zombie, and am trying to say my goodbyes to Heather. The universe still rags on me. What did I ever do to it?

"Jeff!" I hear him scream, now, and his footfalls on the pavement are coming closer, faster and faster.

I stop and lower my shoulders in defeat.

"Hey man, I didn't think I'd catch you," Dante says. He doubles over, panting from his run to catch me.

Good, I hope he hyperventilates.

"What?" I ask curtly.

"Wanna play some ball tonight? I got a crew comin' in from the old neighborhood, and I wanna show'em how we ball up here in mid-town."

"Dante, I want you to look at my ankle."

I watch his eyes move down my leg.

"Oh Jesus! You got bit by a zee?"

"I did," I say, and look at my watch, "and forty-six minutes left before I kind of die. Looks like you're gonna have to count me out of the game tonight."

"Damn, that's a cryin' shame. You the best white baller I know up here man, and I don't think a zee would be cool on the court bro. Well, I guess the shit you got there is for Heather?"

"Yep, one last time to make it up to her."

"God speed brother," he tells me and sticks out his hand

We give each other one last handshake, and he draws me close in a brotherly hug. For a moment, I see the veins pulsing in his neck, and a weird compulsion to tear into his throat washes over me. I give him one last, hard hug, and back off quickly. The scent of his flesh hangs in the air around us, and I try not to, but I lick my lips. I know he saw it too.

"Yeah, well later bro," Dante says, and backs away fast.

He hurries off and doesn't look back. Will he miss me? Only when the boys are coming up for a game, and he needs a good perimeter shooter.

Forty-one minutes.

I try to pick up my pace, but my legs are like trees. I can't bend them very well, and my walking pace becomes damn near a shamble. I hope I don't walk like them until after I turned, but I guess the body doesn't wait. That's ok, though. I only have two blocks to go, and then I'm home free. I can give Heather these last tokens of my love and devotion, and apologize for never getting around to buying her the ring she deserved to get from me.

One more block. Thank God, because I don't think my knees can take any more of this walking stuff. Maybe I won't care how it feels when I'm dead. That would be sweet. Looking around, I pass by a couple holding hands, and I can see the stars in their eyes.

Heather, I'm sorry. I wish I could make those stars appear in your eyes again. If only the same smile I saw on that girl's mouth could cross yours again, I could die happy.

Well, kind of die. You get the picture.

Thirty-two minutes till dead time.

The door to our apartment high-rise has never looked this inviting, and I never noticed the stone angels that stand guard on the corners of the building's entrance. Strange, how when we are about to lose it all, we appreciate it all. I wave to the doorman, and he gives me a half wave in return. Honestly, I've never acknowledged his existence before.

A wave of coughing makes my body quake, and the lobby swims around me. I'm so close to seeing her and holding her. I just want to curl up next to her, and smell the lilac shampoo in her hair, and the soft, apricot aroma from her lotion. Would my hands obey me in those last minutes as I caress her soft skin and cup my hands around the curve of her hips?

I need to hurry.

I want to be gone before I draw my last breath and turn.

Twenty-eight minutes to go, and I stand before the elevator. Punching the up button, I see the little yellow post-it note stuck to the elevator door.

Out of Service. Please Use Stairs. Sorry for the Inconvenience.

Good one, universe; you got me again.

Ok, five floors to go. I hurry to the stairs about as fast as a dying man can go, and throw open the door. Mr. Kennedy, from 5-D, almost gets the door in his face as I push past him and lumber up the stairs. If I could still run, I would. Hell, I would've started running blocks ago so I could have a few more minutes with Heather. Instead, I now have to trudge up the stairs, and hope my legs can hold out.

One flight done, and my body is killing me. I know it is literally killing me, but my limbs are trembling, and I feel my internal temperature rising. Sweat drips from my pores, and the cardboard box housing her chocolates is damp with my perspiration. I check my watch again, but my vision is beginning to blur. I'm not sure if it's from the sweat, or if my pupils are starting to turn milky-white like the zombies, or the 'zees' as Dante calls them.

Fifteen minutes, and one more floor to go.

Each step sends a searing pain through my nervous system. My joints burn, and my blood feels like liquid fire running through my veins. I'm so close to seeing her; I can't stop now. My head keeps ticking to the side. Damn it, a few more stairs to touch her again.

Heather.

I reach the door, and if read my watch right, I have five minutes left. Where did the time go? Guess I'm trudging along slower than I thought. It's getting harder and harder to keep my thoughts straight.

I open the door and enter our apartment, the place we built our love and our life together.

Then I hear it. I hear her cries of ecstasy, and the familiar squeak of our box springs. The musk of sex hangs heavy in the air. Well, that explains her compulsion to always spray air freshener in the apartment before I get home. Oh yeah, she thought I wasn't coming home till late tonight.

Surprise, baby!

Son of a bitch, that's my brother's jacket hanging over the recliner. Did I ever suspect it? I might have, but I was too busy to notice.

The flowers fall from my hand to the floor. I pitch the chocolates, and check the clock on the wall.

Three minutes.

I'm just going to have a seat on the sofa and wait.

I hear them finish and get up.

Good try, but I made her scream more than that, little brother.

Growing hungry. Oh, it gnaws deep in my stomach, and it hurts.

She walks into the living room, looking beautiful, wearing one of my old tee shirts and nothing else. I can't believe my brother got to feel those long, tanned legs.

My brother is a... ass... brains.

Two minutes.

"Jeff! It's not what it looks like."

I know my brother speaks those words, but all I hear is Heather asking me if I feel all right. Her voice caresses my ear with the sound of a traitorous angel.

One minute.

They both come closer, and I feel her soft touch on my sweat-drenched forehead.

"You're burning up," I hear her say with concern, and I grab her arm to touch her one last time

Zero

She... beautiful... I... love... braaaiiinnnns.

***

STORY NOTES:

I wrote this one specifically for a submission call. The project fell through, but I like this story and wanted to share it. The anthology

idea was that zombies are in our society and there is a test kit to see how long you had before you would turn if you were bitten. When I thought about it, I knew if I were bitten, I'd go on an apology tour until my time was up. I also wanted to add some humor in the mix, but I make up for it in the end.

THE CONVERSATION

Brantley brushed the snow from the stone bench and sat down next to the old man.

"Hey papa, been a while," he said as his breath bellowed out in a white cloud into the frigid January air.

"Hell, I know it has boy! Good to see ya'," he answered, flashing Brantley his trademark quirky smile.

"You feeling better yet?"

"Yeah, yeah I guess so. The cancer seems worse on some days then on others," he said, his voice more serious. "So, what brings you out here?" He took a long drag from his cigarette and blew it out into the falling snow.

"I came to tell you I'm sorry. I know I haven't been around, but it killed me to see you suffer. Man, its cold out here papa."

"You get used to it the longer you sit in it. The body can adapt to quite a lot of things, look at me," he said and beat on his chest like an ape.

Brantley laughed and shivered, "I really miss you. I thought I made a mistake coming the last time I saw you, but I'm glad I came by the house now."

"I know you came and watched over me in the hospital during my treatments and I thank you boy. It helped me get through."

"Can I ask you something?"

"Sure boy."

"Did it hurt?"

"The cancer? Hell, yes it did! There were days I wanted to die. Sometimes I just wanted someone to stop by to check on me," he said, a tear forming in his eye.

Brantley broke down and sobbed, "I'm sorry! I couldn't take seeing you like that, it killed me to watch you waste away!"

"It killed me you didn't visit, your mamma needed the help," he answered with his voice choking up, "but, I forgive you."

Grandfather and grandson stood up from the bench and embraced tightly. Each one whispered their love to the other.

"Well, time to go Brantley."

Brantley looked down to the new fallen snow at his feet and whispered, "I know."

Like a small child, Brantley reached out and grasped his papa. Hand in hand they walked down the tree lined path, through the snow, and into the dusk.

***

Clyde Robbins pulled up along the path on his way out to lock the gate and call it a night. Getting out of his truck, he trudged up to the mound of snow forming around a bench and kicked it. Something underneath the drift stopped his boot. Leaning over, he brushed off the top of the snow mound and saw the shoe. Frantically, he swept away the rest of the piled flakes and found a blue face, frozen in death, staring back at him. The dead eyes caught him and before he could scream, he heard laughter.

Turning toward the sound, he saw two people walking together along the back edge of the cemetery. The figures embraced and looking back at Clyde, waved. He watched them carry on and slowly fade from sight as they reached the tree line at the end of the path.

Bending over, he brushed the snow from the bench.

Bruce Thomas Nally

Beloved Husband

Father

Grandfather

May We Be Rejoined

***

STORY NOTES:

I bled for this story. Every raw emotion Brantley expresses is me talking. Losing my grandfather to lung cancer wounded me so deeply that I've never been able to fully heal from it. One night, I sat down and thought about what I would say to him if he walked in and sat beside me. This story grew from that and gave me some comfort having this conversation with him. It was written for a flash fiction anthology and I wanted it to be longer, but by the time I reached the five hundred word limit, I was done. The story was quickly accepted and is the single most painful thing I've written to date.

RIVALS

Todd James slowly opened his eyes. The light hanging above blinded him, so he quickly shut them again. He was lying down somewhere strange, but had no idea where. He tried to get up. His mind rolled over, but his body remained on its back. He thought his body was being rather stubborn, because he didn't drink much, if he remembered correctly, so it wasn't the booze. Todd tried to wrap his mind around his current situation. He couldn't deny the fact he was someplace he didn't know with no idea how he got there.

He remembered talking to the cute blonde girl at Al's Pub. She giggled at his jokes and drank greedily of the beer and shots he bought her. He told her about his summer job as a male dancer, trying to use that combined with the booze to woo her into the sack. After an hour, she agreed to go to his place and they quickly paid the tab and headed outside. The girl was so inebriated that when they exited out the backdoor, she fell over. Todd reached out to catch her and she fell through his hands, slamming down onto the cold pavement. Laughing, he bent over to help her up and suddenly the world went black.

Todd laid there and listened. Since his ears were the only thing besides his eyes working, he tried using them to figure out what happened to him. He wondered if the girl was in on it. Was it a cult? A group of weird junkies or sex slavers? Todd hoped they didn't want to sell his organs on the black market.

He thought he heard something besides him, so he tried to look that way. Todd cursed to himself when he found his gaze still locked upwards at the white light. He heard the scurrying of something behind him. He hated mice, rats, and any other rodent. In fact, the thought of them freaked him out. A cold chill tried to make its way down his spine, but he couldn't even feel that, so he imagined what it would feel like. After thinking about it for a minute, Todd decided he wouldn't have liked how it felt.

His thoughts settled back on his current situation. Whiskey couldn't have done this to him, so he concocted a theory he must have been drugged. His shallow breathing stayed low and even, his fear of the rats (or mice) couldn't even bring a response from his body. Todd closed his eyes and tried to ignore the sounds of little claws on the floor around him. His heart rate began racing. Then he heard the voices, two of them, and getting louder.

"We were lucky we got a guy and a girl at the same time," said the first voice.

"My plan worked perfectly," answered the second voice.

Since Todd could not see them he tried to separate their voices in his mind. The first one that spoke had a deeper tone and the second spoke with a slightly higher pitch and a Jersey accent.

"Wait a minute, I came up with the plan first!" exclaimed Deep.

"You did, I just executed it faster than you," answered Jersey with a smugness.

"Hey, I've been in this business a lot longer than you, so you can piss off."

"Relax; I thought we were in this together? Partners, friends?"

The talking stopped and Todd could hear some metal objects banging and clanking around beyond where his toes were sticking up. He made another futile effort to raise his head so he could get a look at the two disembodied voices he heard. When his head stayed down again, he tried to grunt out an acknowledgement of his failure, but nothing came out except the barely noticeable trace of his breath. The patter of little feet continued their dance around his head. He held his breath and tried to roll his head over to the side and once again he found himself staring straight up. The parade around his head continued.

"Ok, you know the drill. We each have four turns to do something dreadful to our person. Once each round is over, we will ask the third bound person who won the round. When the fourth round ends, we will tally the score and see who the winner is," Jersey explained.

Deep's voice rose in anger, "You know we could've avoided this if you hadn't put our rivalry in the public eye. I was fine until the last hooker I killed got pinned on you. You always take my credit!"

"Look, to show what a sport I am, I'll let you go first. I wasn't my fault though. What did you expect me to do, go to the police and tell them they blamed the wrong serial killer? Let's just get on with it," Jersey said in a stuck up sneer.

Todd heard the metal clanking again. One set of footsteps approached on his right and the tiny feet approached on the left. He figured the girl from the bar was the woman they were referring to. Todd's body didn't work, but his mind at least still functioned, so the other person being the girl was a pretty good guess. The man using the loud, clanking instrument grunted and a wet ripping sound followed.

"Wow, are you really going to start with the old 'eat the kidney' trick? No wonder you always have to copy me, you've got no game of your own," Jersey said with a slightly condescending tone.

"Really, are you going to bring that up? I thought we were passed that."

"No, no, go right on ahead, I won't bring up that night in Florida. In fact, I'm going to let you take all your turns now. Finish whatever you're going to do."

Todd closed his eyes and prayed. That bought him some more time. Maybe, just maybe, the drug would wear off before Jersey turned his attention to him. A loud slurping sound filled his ears as he imagined Deep chewing on the liver. It made him feel ill because as a child, his grandfather tried to make him eat cow liver and he vomited it back on his grandfather's shoes. Todd stayed away from eating all animal organs ever since.

The knife or whatever instrument of destruction Deep used fell to the floor and Todd heard him dig for another tool. Another round of slicing and wet smacks followed as parts from the other person fell to the floor and splattered on impact. Todd felt his stomach sink. He wondered if the recent flurry of activity was just one move in the game or the end.

Jersey's voice broke the men's silence, "Eating a kidney, gnawing on a bone, and just popping out and eye and eating it? Damn man, I was hoping for some sort of contest here and you were just kind of average."

"Screw you!" Deep mumbled while ocular jelly ran out of the corners of his mouth.

"Wait, what are you doing? Why are you moving her legs like that? Ok, fine, that grossed me out. Let's get your final score from our judge. The jury says…" Jersey let the sentence hang in the air as he flung his arm at the man tied in the chair. Like a game show host bringing attention to door number one. He stopped suddenly, "Damn, he's dead."

Jersey picked up the man's arm and it dropped back down to the corpse's side. He shrugged and turned back around.

"What now smartass?" asked Deep.

"My turn," Jersey sang, stepping over to the container of tools and other sharp objects.

Todd tried to scream, but could not. The drug still held its sway over him and his silent scream went nowhere. He could hear the footsteps and the banging. It grew louder in his ears and a ringing started. In an instant, the banging stopped. Jersey's footsteps came closer and closer. Todd knew the end had come. He closed his eyes and focused his mind on moving. His mind grunted and pushed, trying to force his arms or legs to move. He opened his eyes back up and saw a silver glint over his head. It moved down slowly and touched his forehead. He imagined the cold feel of the metal against his flesh and screamed in his mind.

The rodents scampered around Todd again and a bead of sweat dripped down his forehead.

Jersey paused for a moment, "What do we have here?"

Silent minutes passed and until he heard the metal blade slide up and down the table he laid on. Todd pictured all the parts he might be missing now and how much blood he lost. The blade clanged on the table again and fell silent. The footsteps circled the table and came back to Todd's head. A flash of fur flew past his face and the sounds of the feet around him thundered in his ears like elephants. His heart hammered in his chest and his breath quickened as a rat parked its body on his face. Todd glimpsed the blade high above his head, swinging down in one final arc.

For Todd, the world permanently went black with one last silent scream.

***

"Holy shit, I think you killed him!" shouted Deep.

"Of course I did. What'd ya expect from me?" asked Jersey, placing the knife back in the box.

"But man, you never touched him! Never cut him once! Nice use of a rat though, throwing it on his face that way."

"I win, so the first round is on you," said Jersey while they grabbed their coats, flipped off the lights, and shut the doors.

***

STORY NOTES:

Here is the piece I penned for the Cemetery Dance short story contest. It is an early piece too and I was happy it placed third in a really tough group. Some groups were light, but mine featured one of the winners and I felt honored to have mine do as well as it did in the voting. I have cleaned it up from the original and it is a little longer now. This was my first time trying to inject a touch of humor into my work and this is my ode to Jeff Strand.

Beneath

"Come on Nick," his brother Franklin taunted and threw the empty beer can on the ground.

"Come on Nick what?" Sherrie giggled and took a long drag from the cigarette she coyly kept hanging out of her mouth.

"My baby brother is afraid of the dark, Sherrie!" Franklin slapped his knee and burst out in a loud obnoxious laugh.

Nick sank back in his camping chair and quietly took a long drink from his flask.

"Afraid of the dark? Like a little kid?" Sherrie inquired and flicked her cigarette butt into the camp fire.

"Fuck you, Franklin," Nick muttered and gave him the finger.

"Hey, I don't blame you in a way, but it made sharing a room with you as kids hard as hell at night. Sherrie, we had to have lights on in our room all the time after what happened at our grandparent's house," Franklin explained.

"So, what happened?" Sherrie asked. Her tone lost its mocking edge and she sounded interested in Nick's story.

"I really don't want to talk about it," Nick whispered and started to get up from the chair. "Now, if you'll excuse me, I have to take a leak."

Nick turned his back and walked a few feet to the edge of the clearing where their tents were pitched. The moon and the blazing campfire lit the woods enough he could feel safe. A few shadows lingered around him from the trees, but the warm orange glow kept his fear at bay. Undoing his zipper, he whistled a short tune and went about his business while the others laughed and carried on behind him.

I know their laughing at me, he thought. *Honestly, I would too if I were them.*

Finished, he gave it a few shakes and zipped back up before returning to the fire. Franklin sat with his arm wrapped around Sherrie and they both cackled, doubled over and in tears from laughing so hard.

"You two can go to Hell," Nick said and stifled back a laugh of his own trying to look tough and not like an adult who still slept with the lights on when the sun went down. Truth was however, they were right to laugh and he knew it.

"Look, what are you doing next weekend?" Franklin asked and stood up.

"There's nothing that I can think of off-hand. Why?"

"We weren't doing anything either, so let's take a quick trip to the old place and see the cave again."

"Why the fuck would I want to do that? That place screwed me up so bad, I'm still not right. Remember the therapy after Josie left me? Well, that bitch told me the same thing, that I need to 'confront my fears' and shit," Nick lashed out clearly frustrated.

Franklin held his hands up and backed away for a moment. "I'm going to go in with you brother. I only want to help you."

Memories swam around in Nick's head; the night in the cave, his irrational fear of the dark, and Josie leaving him because of his issues.

Maybe it will work, going back there with Franklin.

"Ok, I'll do it," Nick said sounding dejected. He slumped his shoulders in defeat and plopped back in his chair.

Damn it, I let him do it to me again. He always pushes me around.

"You will?" Sherrie sounded surprised.

"Of course he will! He wants to grow up and be big and strong like me!" Franklin teased and inhaled the rest of his beer. "We'll get you fixed up brother."

In the dying fire light, Nick began to feel the world creep in around him and he started to wonder if he made the right choice. Watching the fire, it popped and he followed the flight of the embers as they burned brightly and then were snuffed out in the night. Holding his flashlight tight, he turned it on and prayed morning would hurry and arrive.

***

The next week, the wood's silence was broken as the four-wheelers came to a halt beside the old rusted bars in the side of the moss covered hill. Vines grew up and wrapped themselves around the bars. The entrance appeared untouched and forgotten. Both men dismounted and stood before the locked entrance to the cave. Nick fished around in his pocket and pulled out the butane lighter Josie bought him for his birthday before the split. She hoped it would be a symbol of their relationship, but the hold the darkness held on him wouldn't release him from its grasp. He glanced over to make sure Franklin wasn't looking and he slipped into the backpack his older brother packed for him.

"Doesn't look like anybody's been here since we were kids," Nick mused and gently ran his fingers across the brown sun-dried vines.

"Honestly, I haven't even thought about this place since that day. Hell, I can't even think who put the gate across the opening."

"Maybe old man Helfrich did."

"Yeah, but you saw how overgrown the trail was, this place hasn't been touched in years," Franklin added.

"It's like it was wiped from the town's memory, but why?"

Franklin slapped Nick on the shoulder and laughed, "Wiped from memory? Brother, that's funny! You sound like you believe in that magic bullshit the old guys around here talk about."

"Don't you ever wonder?"

"Look, are you ready for this? I'll let you back out if you think you can't handle it," Franklin said sarcastically.

"Just unlock the gate and let's get this over with," he retorted and threw the pack over his shoulder.

Both brothers ripped at the vegetation covering the entrance and cleared away the dying vines. Nick backed away and felt his chest tighten as Franklin turned the key in the rusted locked and tugged on the gate. The weathered hinges groaned and he pulled hard to break the gate free from the mouth of the cave. Behind the gate, another metal door protected the entrance and kept unwanted visitors out of the caverns below. Franklin flipped to the next key and opened it as well.

Nick closed his eyes and tried to fight off the panic building within him. Hearing the creaking gates and knowing what awaited him within in the black set his heart racing. Taking a deep breath, he slowed his panting and calmed himself on the outside. The inside was another matter.

"You ready?" Franklin asked.

"Let's go," Nick answered and turned on his flashlight.

"After you," Franklin smiled and motioned to the entrance.

Nick turned and took a step toward the threshold when he stopped. Beyond the doorway, beyond the reach of the sun's light was the darkest black he'd seen in years, the darkest since the last time he ventured into the cave on his grandparent's land...

The last time when at age twelve, his world went black and changed him.

Now he timidly stood at the precipice and gazed into his salvation. Ahead, in the cave he could be cured. Ahead, he would wrap himself in the darkness and overcome his paralyzing achluophobia. Inhaling deeply, he stepped past the threshold and inside the cave.

Nick gingerly ran his fingers along the cold damp walls and rubbed the mud between his fingers. Behind him, he heard Franklin enter and stop behind him.

"We're not in the dark yet, keep walking."

Nick's heart raced and it thundered, threatening to explode from his chest. "Just… just, give me a minute."

"What happened down here anyway? You used be a normal kid," Franklin said.

"I can't quite remember. Every night when I lay down and try to sleep, I can feel it try to surface, but then the night freaks me out and I turn the lights on. Josie hated it when I turned them on every night. We settled on a nightlight, but there were too many dark places in our bedroom. Places it could hide," Nick whispered.

"What could hide?"

"I don't know and that's the fucking point Franklin! I don't fucking know!" The whisper in his voice rose in rage at his brother's questions.

"Ok, ok…" Franklin responded and held his hands up in a gesture of surrender.

Nick gripped his flashlight tighter and took another step into his personal abyss. He gathered as much courage as he could muster, his step turned into two and his two to three until he found himself past the opening and into the first chamber. He paused momentarily until he heard his brother's footsteps fall in behind him.

"He we are, the main entry chamber," Franklin said. He placed his hands on Nick's shoulders and gave him a reassuring squeeze.

"I remember coming in here to hide from Grandpa. I broke Grandma's vase and he chased me out of the house with the old horse whip."

"He did that? Shit, I always heard him threaten me with it, but he never grabbed out of the closet."

Nick's eyes roamed the chamber and his flashlight beam splashed across the brown walls. He followed the water trails from the ceiling to the floor and the cave's coolness began to make his flesh prickle up.

"Grandpa stopped. He yelled at me to come back, but then he stopped chasing me," Nick said and turned his head toward Franklin. "He looked afraid."

"Bullshit, Grandpa wasn't afraid of anything. He was the bravest guy in White Creek," Franklin answered indignantly.

"Yeah, but something about this place stopped him cold. I couldn't believe it because he ran after me so angry. He'd never been like that before."

"So, you're starting to remember now?"

"Weird, I haven't been able to think about anything from that day, and now it's like a flood in my head."

"What's ahead?"

"I think there is another chamber like this through that opening over there," Nick answered and pointed to a gap in between two large rock faces.

"After you," Franklin grinned.

Nick closed his eyes for a moment to focus on keeping his cool. He tried to take a step, but his foot felt glued to the wet ground. Tensing up, he forced his legs to move and steadily began to walk toward the opening.

Each step further into the cave made his breath came in quick short pants. He felt anxiety race through him and panic grew the closer he came to the opening.

"Come on! Remember, the best way to overcome your fear is to face it head on and kick its ass," Franklin said encouraging him to move on.

Nick poked his head into the dark room and shined his flashlight around. He saw a large open area with a drop off on the left and a small hole in the rock face straight ahead.

Franklin's hands pushed on Nick's back and he stumbled forward into the black room. His knee struck the stone floor and the flashlight bounced from his hand and rolled to the left. Franklin laughed behind him and the echoes of his footfalls grew farther and farther away.

"Never go alone!" his brother's voice sneered at him.

The light from the entrance chamber shortened and he heard the rusted door swing shut, plunging him in darkness.

The single beam of light from the flashlight lit his path and he started to crawl to retrieve it. His knee ached from the fall and he paused.

"That son of a bitch," he murmured.

The flashlight leaned to the left and rolled again.

"Shit," he muttered as he heard the flashlight bounce down the crevasse.

For a few moments, he could see the light move from side to side as it dropped further and further into the cave's gullet. Each time the flashlight hit on the sides, he cringed at the sound it made and the way the light beams moved wildly around. At some point, he saw the last bit fade away before the sound of the metal casing hit the bottom and echoed back up through the hole.

Nick sat in the total darkness and tried not to cry.

In the cave's blackness, he felt around in his pocket for his phone. Feeling the familiar rectangle shape, he pulled it out and turned it on. The screen lit up with life and Nick shined it around the room he sat in. Before the flashlight slipped from his damp fingers, he made mental note of the small opening on the far side of the cave.

"Do I go back or do I move forward?" he asked himself. His voice echoed around the chamber and he sighed. Dread began to creep into his thoughts and the dark started to make him feel jittery.

I shouldn't have listened to Franklin. "Never go alone", he said before he pushed me in here with the pack and nothing else. Well, I fucked up for trusting him; he thought and noticed his phone had only ten percent left on the battery.

Quickly, he shut it off and felt around in the pack they left him with again. He felt through the granola bars, the extra ropes, and then he found the cold metal shape he'd been looking for; the lighter he slipped in before entering. Carefully retrieving it from his pack as not to drop it, he pulled it out and held the lighter to his cheek. In the dark, its touch felt comforting while everything else around him closed in on him.

When Nick flipped open the top and flicked the flint, it sprang to life and the orange flame cast a soft glow in the black. The flame danced on the wick and a sickening realization hit him.

He hadn't refilled it in a month or so.

His elation at finding it cooled and the cave's temperature caused him to shiver. He closed the lighter's top and sat unmoving in the cave chamber as the black swallowed him again.

"Same place as before. Do I go back or do I move forward," he whispered to himself.

He waited for his voice to echo in the chamber, but he whispered so quietly, nothing answered him back.

It was in the next room, through the small hole.

A quick memory flashed in his mind and he tried to focus on it, to bring it back so he could remember. Instead, the thought fled him and he was left with his thoughts on the dark again.

The temperature froze him and he imagined his breath bellowing out in front of him in the dark. Rubbing his hands over his arms, he tried to warm himself.

"Jacket would have been nice."

It quickly became harder and harder to breath. Around him, he felt the black squeeze him and tighten its grip. Even though the cave was cold and Nick shivered, a sweat broke out and droplets ran down his face.

Nick.

He stopped and held his breath. Through the dripping water and the sound of his racing heart, he swore he heard his name on the breeze in the cave.

Nick.

His blood turned to ice in his veins. The voice sounded familiar, like something he'd heard in a dream.

Or something I'd heard the last time I came here, he thought and turned his cell phone on.

The screen's light illuminated a small area of space around Nick and it formed a bubble around him to keep the dark at bay. Surrounded by the faint light, he began to feel better. Not totally fine, but good enough his mind could function clearly.

Last time, I came in here. I wasn't afraid. The dark didn't scare me. What happened next?

He held his phone up and shined it around the cavern. Once again, he stopped on the small hole at the far end. Checking his phone, he saw he only had three percent of the battery charge left.

"Well, here we go," he said to the gloom and shut his phone off.

Gingerly, he started to crawl across the muddy ground. The rocks dug into his hands and knees. Small pieces of stone imbedded themselves in his skin and pressed hard with each movement forward.

Nick.

He stopped. His limbs refused to respond to him and terror swept through him again. He turned the phone back on and realized he only moved a few feet. Around him, he noticed the dripping water had ceased. Everything around him was completely silent. Only his breathing filled the chamber. Slowing his breaths, he surveyed the distance again and the phone went dead plunging the chamber into absolute darkness again.

Nick.

Nick took one motion forward and felt something different under his hand. The ground was slicker and tacky like glue. Fighting the urge to scream, he stifled it back and proceeded to make his way to the hole.

There wasn't the door to the cave and I had a little bit of light to see by. I saw the ravine to the left and threw rocks down in it so I could listen to them bounce off the sides and echo in the large chamber. Then I heard something by the hole. I looked over and I saw a light in the next room. I stopped throwing rocks and went over there.

The train of memories barreling through his skull stopped and suddenly derailed. The panic building in him froze him again.

"Wait a minute," he muttered and fished the lighter out.

Nick slipped his shoe off and fired the lighter up. The orange flame danced and he laid it on his shoe strings. The nylon laces ignited and the shoe caught fire, blazing in the cave. He recalled seeing something on a survival show about the soles on the shoe being able to smolder for some time. Even if it burned to just embers on the rubber soles, he would take any light he could get.

Something happened in the next room and I can't remember. Something changed me. Something is still there; he thought and slid himself forward.

Once he began moving again, his hands stuck to the ground and ripped them free of the mud with every motion. The mud created a suction that sealed his palms to the clay muck. Nick pushed the shoe forward and then took another slow agonizing crawl behind it. The ground beneath him dried up a little and with his hands not being glued to the ground with each push, he made up ground.

"Shit," he muttered and glanced behind him.

In the flickering light, he saw the backpack still back near the ravine's edge. The dripping resumed again and he stared at the pack, hoping it would miraculously appear closer to him. Instead, it remained in the spot where he left it, surrounded by the encroaching shadows and the black. The shoe fire dimmed and the pack was consumed by the dark.

Hope I don't need it, he thought and pushed on.

Nick.

The voice called out in the gloom again. This time, he knew it came from the hole before him. Searching his head, he tried to think about what happened beyond the hole. What did he find that scared him so bad he couldn't stand to be in the dark?

Nick stopped and listened closely for the voice. Then realization hit him.

The fear wasn't crippling him. His heart still hammered in his chest and his breathing still came in short panicked bursts, but the sense of fear and dread he felt slowly evaporated. Emboldened, Nick pressed on. Confidence rushed through him and he reached the hole in a few minutes. Looking back across the cavern, he was amazed by his progress.

Nick. Come to me. You belong here.

The words struck him like an uppercut to the chin.

I've come so far. I have to keep moving. I know the therapist said that immersing myself in my fear could help me overcome it and so far I think what Franklin did id helping me. I don't feel as threatened by the dark as I did, but the voice. What is it with the voice? I belong here? What does that mean? He thought and used a rock to shove the burning shoe into the hole.

He heard the shoe drop down and land hard on the rock floor below. Leaning forward, he stuck his head in the hole and scoped out the room.

"Ok, not a straight forward room, but a drop to the next one."

Wiggling on his stomach, he started to snake his way head-first down the hole. Halfway through, the hole became smaller and Nick felt the stone constrict around him the further he tried to go. Feeling his arm get blocked, the pressure built in his chest and the fear filled him again. Below him, the shoe's glow began to die away and the chamber below him grew darker.

"Shit."

Carefully, he backed out a few inches and put his arm above his head so he could squeeze through the opening. In the shadows below, he saw movement against the wall. Quickly, he pushed his body harder and forced his midsection through the hole like he was passing through the eye of a needle. He fell from the opening and landed hard on the rock floor. The force of his landing forced the air from his lungs and his shoulder flared up in pain. Grimacing in agony, he turned his head to watch the shoe flicker one last time before the flame disappeared and left him in the darkness.

Something dragged along the ground ahead of him. The hair on the back of his neck stood up and a chill shot up his spine. The noise repeated itself and it moved closer to Nick. His pulse raced and the progress he thought he made retreated leaving him afraid again.

Nick.

His fear drove down on him like a weight and the thing slid closer, the sound reminding him of sandpaper dragging across a piece of wood.

Nick. Remember me.

Nick closed his eyes and tried to ignore the voice, but it rang his head and he went deep in his thoughts wanting to remember that summer.

I came down here. There was a light. I heard something like water, rushing water. Then... the skulls.

Nick, join us.

"Who are you?" he screamed, the force of his voice surprising him.

Silence answered.

"Answer me damn you!" he bellowed.

The light. Join us and leave the light. We've been waiting for you.

Nick pulled out his lighter and flicked in on. The flame roared to life and faltered, its butane running low. He waved the lighter around slowly so he could find the source of the noise in the corner. The dragging continued, but he didn't see anything.

"Who's there? Show yourself!"

The flame flickered and became a dull blue. Slowly, the flame devoured the last drops of butane from the wick and died. Once the cavern became pitch black again, the sounds multiplied. The dragging surrounded him and he lost himself. The fear overwhelmed him and he let out a primal scream into the abysmal cave. His shriek echoed throughout the caverns and his maniacal laughter followed it.

Then he heard it, the sound of trickling water followed by a splash. In the dark, he couldn't see, but he let his ears guide him through the dark. All around him, he pictured smiling demons and skeletons grabbing at him and each rock he placed his hand on became a bone or monster in his mind. A breeze blew through the cavern and the sound of the water grew closer.

Don't leave us again. Release us from our prison.

"Get out of my head!" he cried out and scrambled faster to the water.

He crawled over a large rock and rays of light broke through the ceiling and lit up a patch to a stream rushing through the cave.

"Breeze, water, light… way out," he babbled and stood up.

No, you are ours!

The voice became a chorus around him and something pushed past him.

"I saw you before."

You escaped us before. We waited for you to return to free us like you promised.

"I couldn't free you."

We waited in the dark for you, our reach finding you when the sun moved from the sky.

"Why me?"

Your family trapped us here.

"Why me?"

We need your blood to break the binds.

Nick looked back at the stream and then back at the form swirling in the darkness. Even in the black, the shape seemed to be darker than the blackest night, a complete absence of light.

"No," Nick whispered and fell backward. His body splashed in the stream and the current carried his body a few feet out of the cave and back out into the woods.

Nick climbed from the water and rolled onto his back in a pile of dead leaves. The sun shined upon his face and he soaked up the light and the warmth he felt from it.

Things are going to be different now. I guess I should go and tell Franklin his 'therapy' worked, Nick thought and sat up.

***

"Do you think he's ok?" Sherrie asked.

"I hope so," Franklin said and shrugged his shoulders. He really wanted her to shut up. Since she found him an hour ago, she hadn't shut up about Nick and the drastic measure he took to help cure his brother's fear of the dark.

"What happened to him in cave when you were kids?"

"Hell if I know. There's some local legend about some demons or spirits or something being trapped in there. Grandpa never went in because he knew it wasn't safe and he forbid us from getting near it."

"Why?"

"So we wouldn't fall and die in the dark? Fuck, I don't know," he said irritated.

Behind them a branch snapped and they turned around.

Nick stood before them wet, muddy, and blood running from gashes on his hands and knees. He wore only one shoe and his exposed foot was a bloody mess from walking through the cave and the woods.

"Oh my God, are you ok Nick?" Sherrie said and got up from the tree stump she sat on.

"Did it work?" Franklin asked. A smirk crossed his face.

"I'm not afraid of the dark anymore," Nick muttered.

"Sweet, it worked!" Franklin exclaimed and raised his arms in victory.

Sherrie saw it first, but couldn't react in time. Franklin didn't notice the club-like piece of wood in Nick's hand until he swung it through the air like a baseball bat and smashed it into the side of his face. Franklin fell to the ground and laid their unconscious. Sherrie turned to run, but Nick jumped over his brother's prone body and slammed the branch into the back of her head. She spun around and saw him swing again. Before her world went black, she saw the vacant look in his eyes and strange smile creeping across his face.

***

Franklin opened his eyes and he still saw only darkness. Something moaned beside him and he felt around on the ground. His fingers found a hand and he could feel the familiar ring on Sherrie's finger.

"Sherrie! Sherrie, wake up," Franklin said and shook her. His voice sounded on the verge of tears and fear poured in his tone.

Franklin. Sherrie. You are our sacrifice. You are our release.

"Who's there? Answer me!" Franklin screamed and felt the cave grow colder.

Break the binds with your blood.

Both of them screamed when the air pressure around them changed and began crushing them. Franklin felt the blood pour from his mouth and nose. Sherrie cried out beside him and fell silent. In his last moment, he thought he heard Nick's laughter echoing in the cave.

***

STORY NOTES:

"Beneath" is original to this collection and is very deeply rooted in the White Creek mythology I'm building. There are a few references to the other material, but this one is a showcase for some of the spirits imprisoned in the town's land. Over time, the past is going to be revealed and the dots from "In Memoriam" and all the other White Creek tales will be connected. Right now I can say that the founders of the town did some very bad things and their actions stained the town for generations.

The story started out as an examining Nick's fear of the dark, but the cave became something bigger once I began to write it. He was only supposed to be trapped in the dark cave while his childhood fears played out in his head, but after finishing and publishing, "Payment", I wanted to begin the process of having the spirits slowly being freed from their bindings. The longer the spirits were bound to the earth, the more their evil seeped into the town. In the end, White Creek is a huge magnet for evil. I am focusing more on the mythos, so look for more of it in the future.

THE BECOMING

Ben stepped out on the fallen hotel wreckage and scanned the horizon. Six years after a rogue regime in the Middle East launched its warheads into Jerusalem; the morning skyline still looked like it burned. He thought back to the news that the missiles were approaching the US's eastern seaboard and his school evacuated into the subway tunnels. Overhead, the sky's reddish hue hanging over Boston Harbor reminded him of the mornings he rode his bike to school and played in the park until the sky darkened from blue, to red, and to twilight's purples. For miles, all he gazed out at were the burnt out and decaying husks of civilization.

Without realizing it, he scratched the spot on his shoulder where one of the military doctors gave him a booster shot two days ago. The liquid burned his veins like his heart had begun pumping lava through his system. They told the group of teens the shots were to help them adapt to the changes in the environment. Ben understood why, food and shelter was quickly becoming more and more scarce in the underground tunnels. Last week, the military put ration policies in effect to stem the tide of their rapidly depleting food stores.

"Hey Ben, I knew I'd find you up here," the red headed girl said taking her place at Ben's side.

"Oh, hey Lacey," he said and nodded to her. He felt his cheeks redden. Since he met her in the shelter two years ago they'd become friends and he'd developed a crush on her.

"Why do you always come out to this place? You know they tell us it's not safe to wander around out here," Lacey whispered and took Ben's hand. She squeezed it tightly and he returned the small form of affection.

The spot on his shoulder twitched and he dropped her hand to scratch it again. "The place where the doctors gave you your shot, does it bother you any? Mine burns and the itching is fucking terrible. I had to force myself to stop messing with it. Here, check this out," he offered and rolled up his shirt sleeve.

A low gasp escaped Lacey's lips. The skin around the injection site looked puffy and red. A blood and pus mixture dripped in yellow and crimson droplets down his arm. Several deep gouges criss-crossed the tender flesh. Something about the spot didn't sit right with her. The place where she got her injections bothered her, but not to the extent it did Ben.

Quickly, she covered her mouth and muttered, "Oh my Ben. Have you told the meds about it yet? They said the injections were to help us get ready to live up here full time again so we can straighten everything out, but if there are side effects, you have to tell them!"

"I don't have to tell them shit! If they knew, they'd want to, to… I don't know, experiment on me or something!"

"Aren't they doing that now?" she asked shrugging her shoulders.

He reached over and grabbed her arm. His fingers pressed into her injection site and she winced. She tried to hide the pained expression on her face, but Ben noticed.

"Hurts huh?"

"Look," she said pulling away from him, "nightfall is in a few minutes and they're going to shut the vault doors."

He stared at her for a moment and relented, his sudden angry burst subsiding. Ben stood and watched her head to the checkpoint to reenter the underground. He rushed behind her so they wouldn't get shut outside the thick concrete doors built at the mouths of the subway tunnels that kept the radiation from the languishing citizens below.

Hearing the massive doors drag closed behind him, he felt tired and very, very hungry.

***

The sensations were the same as the dreams before, Ben's mind felt blank and he moved like he was on the ground. He only reacted to the burning in his gut and the prickling of his skin. His vision blurred, but he continued to shovel the food into his mouth. The stench assaulted his nose, a mix of rotted fruit, dirt, and piss from the refuse systems; but it tasted like honey. Spoiled juices ran down his chin and his tongue slurped it up from his lips, drinking down the rank liquid. Dragging his arm across his face, he stopped when the bristles scratched his cheeks. Slowly, he dropped his arm down and looked at the food he'd been stuffing his face with.

His stomach lurched and he threw down the trash in his fists. Suddenly, revulsion turned his guts inside out and he doubled over. With a quick twitch, he glanced at his arms and stifled back a scream. Thick, coarse, black hair sprouted from his pores. Reaching up, he ran his fingers over the irritated places on his face and he felt the skins edges pull up from the muscle. Grabbing on to a piece of skin, he ripped it back and his face fell away…

***

"You look like shit Ben," Lacey noted with her trademark smirk and scratched her shoulder.

"You don't look any better yourself sweetheart," Ben retorted. He studied her as she worked her fingers across her sleeve, trying to rip through the shirt's fabric and tear into the skin beneath. The rash on his arm looked worse than it did when he woke up. It blistered and the coloration reminded him of a lobster fresh from the pot.

"Asshole, you don't tell a girl that! Where are your manners?" she said and playfully punched his arm.

Ben didn't respond directly. His eyes stared blankly out across the dining area where the residents of Boston Shelter A-4 march in to get their morning ration of stale bread and dirty water. The debris floating in the drink reminded him of the fish food he'd give his goldfish when he was a kid. Throwing in the aquarium's top, he watched it float to the bottom and land atop the rainbow colored gravel. The soldiers told them it was safe to drink. He refused at first, but eventually the thirst overtook reason and he greedily gulped down the first glass they handed him. Then they approached him about the program and explained his life would be worth living again on the surface.

"You ah, scratching at the arm a little bit?"

Lacey glanced down and noticed the crimson droplets streaming out from under her sleeve. Turning away, Ben grabbed her and spun her around.

"Having nightmares too? What else aren't you telling me? I thought we had something going," he sneered angrily.

"Yes, I've had terrible nightmares, I think my skin is falling off, and I feel something in my gut that hurts so badly," she yelled and buried her face on Ben's shoulder sobbing.

He patted her head with his hand and caressed her back. Where his fingers ran over the sheer shirt she wore, he felt welts and raised places covering her entire back. Examining her neck, his blood ran cold. The patch of skin looked blackened and small black spines stuck out from her pores. Instinctively, his hand shot to the scruff of his neck, frantically checking his own flesh.

Just below the skin's surface, his fingertips felt the sharp protrusions below the epidermis. A blazing hot flash rushed through his system and he dropped to his knees.

"Oh my God, Ben!" Lacey shouted before a blood-curdling scream exploded from her lungs and she fell to the floor.

Reaching out to grab her hand, Ben heard the claxon blaring up and down the corridor they were in. Pressure built in his ears and his muscles contracted and flexed involuntarily. Cracking, his knees buckled backward and he shrieked in agony. Fighting through the pain, he rolled his head around to check on Lacey.

Her head flopped to the side and her body jerked around in the throes of a seizure. Rips and tears criss-crossed the flesh on her arms and face. Black oozed from her mouth and something tore free of her cheek and flexed outward. The pleas she made were garbled and he couldn't understand what she was trying to say. Her voice sounded like she had a mouth full of cotton trying to speak underwater.

The alarms died off and the cadence of marching boots echoed down the hallway. Blinking trying to clear his eyesight, he saw a man in a bio-suit kneel next to Lacey and inject something in her arm. Trying to shout at the men, something shredded his bottom lip and wiggled in the air. A sharp point slammed into his shoulder and the burning liquid ran up his arm setting all his nerve endings on fire. His head swam and his twisted reflection in the soldier's helmet was the last thing he saw.

***

The dreamland sun blazed across the sky as he roamed the wreckage around Fenway Park where he and his father shared their happiest times. The Green Monster's remains lay in a crumbled heap and the massive outfield Coke bottle had fallen forward, resting in the centerfield weeds. Paper and other debris swirled around the silent empty stadium from the breeze blowing in off the harbor. Around him, Ben heard others clicking around and saw movement in the dugouts and the ruined concession stands.

The stale air reeked of decay, but he found the aroma delicious. Moving across the right field seat, he sniffed around the chipped concrete and licked the faded seats with his tongue. The dirt tasted wonderful and he spied a pile in the corner that looked like popcorn boxes and crushed drink cups. Quickly, he scurried over and reached out to grab the sweet trash.

Grabbing hold, the skin on the back his hand split. His middle two fingers hung limp and folded under the flesh pulling away from his arm. No blood poured from the wounds and the other muscle layer fell from his bones. Turning his head away quickly to avoid looking at his arm, he saw the others in the field.

Trying to vocalize the scream failed. Dropping the trash and bringing his hand up to his face, he shrieked in horror and left the dream world behind.

***

Waking up, the words in his ears were muffled. At first he didn't understand everything, but the conversation around him clarified.

"The experiment is a success doctor?"

"Yes, the two subjects were injected with the recombinant DNA has shown the beginning stages of metamorphosis. Soon, you can deploy them to the surface."

"This had better work."

"I assure you, they will help get the surface prepared for us to leave these damn underground hovels."

"Excellent, the president will be… wait, they're stirring."

Ben relaxed and the fog cleared from his head. The edges of his vision remained blurred and the light above him looked like a prism. He struggled to move his hands so he could wipe his eyes, but he felt them bound to the table he laid on. Squirming around, he noticed his chest was also strapped down.

Focusing as hard as he could, he stared in shock at where Lacey lay strapped to a table. Her fingertips broke open and dark brown claws slid out of her skin. Two shapes ran around her and frantically tried to tighten the leather straps holding her down. An unholy cry erupted from her lips and they broke apart, onyx mandibles pushing the skin away. Her head flopped over and faced Ben.

Her scalp split and her flesh formed cracks down the center of her face. Large feelers grew from underneath her hair and extended into the room and waved wildly around. The mandibles opened and closed like scissors and the skin broke free of her face and sloughed off to either side. Her deep amber eyes gazed at him and a vacant look crossed her new insect face. Ben felt his insides rumble and he knew it was only a matter of time now before his final transformation began.

Lacey's arms tugged at the bindings and broke free. Flailing her arms in the air wildly, her arms fell off her body. Large armored appendages flexed with pointed pinchers opening and closing. A wet ripping came from her midsection and her new body rose from the molted human skin remaining on the table. Rolling back with her shoulders, wings unfurled and she flapped them once. Ben cringed at the sound they made in the air.

The two men in the room screamed and she reached out with her pinchers and grabbed the one in the white lab coat. The claw's serrated edges dug through his coat and tore into his flesh. The white quickly turned red and she jerked her arm hard severing the doctor in half. A crimson spray shot into the air like a geyser and his top half toppled to the ground. Lacey shook his intestines free of her pincher and got to her feet.

The other man stood by the door and pounded on it loudly screaming for someone to open it. Reaching to his holster, he whipped out his pistol and squeezed off three shots into Lacey. The bullets slammed into her thorax and bounced harmlessly to the floor. Pushing down on her thin and barbed legs, she sprang toward the man and buried her mandibles in his neck. The blood showered her head and she drank deep of his life.

Ben heard the familiar sounds of the change emanating from his own body. A cold sweat covered him and the heat in his core rose. Opening his mouth, his jaw dislocated and his face slid backward from his head. Tearing free from his mortal shell, his mind reset to his baser needs. Looking across the room, he saw Lacey drop the soldier's corpse and turn toward him. The only thing his mind recognized was his hunger and his lust.

The two monstrosities scrambled to the middle of the room and embraced. Holding each other, they became aware the temperature rose rapidly. Flames roared from ceiling vents and the cloth covers on the beds burst into flames. The room filled with the aroma of the dead scientist's bodies smoking and cooking in the heat.

Ben and Lacey's eyes met and something flashed through their new insect minds. A brief remembrance from what seemed like a lifetime ago and a final understanding of their fate.

Beneath their new shells, they felt their own insides boil. Lacey reared back and her abdomen exploded from the expanding internal gasses. Ben rolled on the scorching tiles and crawled toward the door. Climbing over the charred doctor's remains, he reached out to the door and then a low guttural moan escaped his mouth. Underneath his exoskeleton, his flesh ignited and flames exploded through his armor. With one last gasp, he turned back toward Lacey and reached out to her outstretched arm. Falling to the floor, his pincher landed in hers and he took his last hot, burning breath.

***

The men stared in the observation window and scribbled down some notes. Inside the room on the other side of the glass, the flames finished consuming the failures. Dying away, the cool down cycle kicked in and the fans blew air in so the clean-up crew could finish eliminating all trace of the experiment.

"What now Dr. Warren?"

"I believe what we are doing is right. If we can perfect the process, combining the cockroach DNA with some of the dead weight around here will allow us to create a workforce for the surface and find food."

"Should we go back to the drawing board?"

"No, find two more for the injections, I believe we are getting close," Dr. Warren noted and closed his notebook. Once his assistant closed the door behind him, he reached down and pulled out a zip drive. Scrolling through the files, he found the details from the president about *Operation: Reclamation* and began to write out his report.

***

STORY NOTES:

This was just a quick and fun romp through a bleak future where the remaining pieces of the government experiment on teens so they can return to the surface. I also played with the bonds love builds between two people and that no matter how bad things get or what they turn into, love will always trump all. Well, love in my twisted voice...

BRENT ABELL

SWEET NOTHINGS

The night was clear and cool as the headlights bathed the front of the Chase house when a car crept into the drive. Daniel put the car in park, grabbed his lunch pail, and snubbed out the last lingering remains of his Camel. He took a deep breath and slowly unfolded himself from the car. Twelve hour days doing grunt work in the emergency room at White General really grated on him. He was glad that coming home was now a relief. It never seemed like much of a refuge before.

After two painful years of marriage, he felt that over the last week they had finally turned a new page in their relationship; the rut he felt they were in had ended. When he came home tired from work and grabbed a beer, Hope no longer bitched. She was now also silent about what he ate, his smoking habit, and leaving the toilet seat up. In fact, the last week with Hope had been the happiest of his wedded life. He actually loved to hurry home to his bride. As Daniel considered his new bliss, a smirk crossed his lips. Soon he would show her how much he really cared.

Hope was rude, haughty, and otherwise demeaning to Daniel. Nothing he did ever pleased her. When he had one beer, he drank too much. When he had an extra slice of pizza, he ate too much. During sex if he finished before her, he was the most selfish prick on the planet. Never mind the fact that she could be more frigid than an iceberg. It took an act of God for him to be allowed to touch her in any romantic manner since their wedding night. To his delight, this too had changed for the better; sex was no longer a special occasion. Things were indeed looking up.

Before their fight, he had often felt like sticking his Smith and Wesson in his mouth and decorating the living room walls with bits of his brain matter and skull fragments. Hope would have been more upset about the cleaning bill then the fact that her husband just ate a bullet because he couldn't stand her. He spent most of his home life in misery and usually he longed for work. She had ultimately crushed his spirit.

Coming home from work last week, Daniel suffered an anxiety attack; one with a name: Hope. He knew that if he were to ever be happy again he would have to confront her. From the moment he set foot in the house until the moment his head hit the pillow on the couch to sleep – he was not allowed in the bedroom that night - he started to defend himself. Hope was beside herself, how dare he have his own thoughts, opinions, and ideas. This was *her* house and this needed to *stop*, before Daniel made a habit of sticking up for himself.

Then they finally had the fight.

The fight was like a bomb had exploded in the house. All the pent up anger and frustration from their entire relationship erupted in a spectacular display of screaming and rage. Before he realized what had happened, he stood bewildered, watching her slide down the door leaving a bloody trail behind her. As he turned her head and saw the damage to her face, he panicked, but then he saw the chance for a better life.

Things had changed and would be forever different.

Daniel opened the door to the kitchen and entered *his* house. It was very dark, and a strange odor filled his nostrils. Glancing over at the sink, he saw that the dishes from the last week were still there. The last few days he had been using the boxes from the pizza he ordered for supper plates. He did at least get the trash out to the curb. Last week he forgot and had to bug spray the trash can to kill the flies and their lovely maggot offspring. Laundry was another matter entirely.

Aiming to be silent, he tiptoed towards the bedroom. Hope was lying on her side of the bed under the sheets. Daniel stood there and watched her. She was as beautiful as always. He pulled off his pants, boxers, and shirt letting them all fall to the floor where he stood. His erection stood at attention and he crawled into bed next to his beloved. Not wanting to wait, he pulled her next to him and started to caress her smooth thighs. Sliding his hand north, he tugged on the hard, dark knobs of her nipples. He rolled her over, took them into his mouth, and flicked them with his tongue. Daniel took his other hand and placed it between her legs and felt for some kind of a response. Just as before, she never elicited any. Grinning madly, he spread her legs and began driving himself into her as hard as he could.

After a few short moments, he unleashed his seed into her and rolled off onto the bed. Facing her, he grabbed her jaw and forced his lips on hers. Satisfied, he rose from the bed and began to put his boxers back on. Daniel looked back to her and he smiled as he noticed a tear silently streaming down her scarred cheek. He considered the marks on her face from their fight her 'love mask'. Making his way to her side of the bed, he checked the IV drip that went into her arm. He hummed quietly to himself as he upped the dosage on the drug cocktail that swam through her veins to keep her unable to move or talk, his perfect wife.

In the past few weeks, Daniel found working at a hospital had its privileges.

***

STORY NOTES:

What you just finished reading was my first story. It's never been published, but it has been read in the public. It was penned for the open mike reading at Mo-Con V in Indianapolis. I sat there and read for my favorite authors and once the twist hit; my favorite author took out a lighter and began waving it back and forth at his table. After the readings and at the after party, he tried to help sell the story, but the story never quite made it in anything. I trunked it and left it to sit, but I decided to place it in here as a comparison to how much my work has changed and evolved over the past few years.

THE REAPER RIDES

1

Matt Thomas looked down at his watch again and muttered an inaudible curse under his breath. For the second time in two weeks he missed the MARC train into Baltimore, so for the second time in two weeks, he was going to be really late for work. The guys at the office always razzed him about living in DC and commuting into Baltimore instead of the other way around. He didn't care; he told them he loved the area and loved politics. He stood lost in his thoughts until the intercom blasted the boarding call for the 8:45 am to Baltimore. Matt stood up from the cold, hard plastic bench, and hurried to the boarding area hoping not to miss this one.

The train took another ten minutes to arrive once Matt reached the platform. The hustle and bustle carried on around him as he tried to listen to a news cast on the TV sets positioned in the station. Reading the words scroll by on the bottom news feed, he made out something about a new flu strain and how they believed weevils carried it this time instead of birds, cows, or pigs. The warmth of summer was slowly fading into early fall's chilly embrace, so the fear mongering about the new 'killer flu bug' was starting to hit its full stride. The picture flashed to a mall in California where everyone was wearing white masks like the Japanese did during the avian flu scare. A young man in front of him was hunched over his cell phone and gasped loudly. Matt looked over the guy's shoulder and was stunned by what he saw on the screen.

Another man came over and caught the tail end of the video the same time Matt did. "What the hell was that? Replay it."

Matt looked back at the man then back to the phone guy, "Yeah, play that again."

The camera in the video focused on a large strange pile in the middle of a village. The image zoomed in and they could see that the pile was full of moving people. The mass of human flesh must have numbered in the hundreds, all writhing together in crying agony. From the camera's right, four men in white biohazard suits moved into the picture, all sporting flamethrowers. Encircling the human mountain, they let loose with the torches and set the pile on fire. The flames spread quickly as the skin and hair of the people caught ablaze. Shrieks of agony and shouts for help echoed from the iPhone's speakers. In the footage, the cameraman tried to move into a better position, but then the camera jolted forward like it was hit from behind. The picture shifted as the camera fell to its side. One of the white suited men approached the camera, getting closer and closer until it caught the image of his boot heel rising up and slamming down. The picture then went to static.

A group of people on the platform had gathered around the phone, disbelieving what they were seeing. The phone was turned outwards so more people could see and others were bringing the video up on their own phones. There had been stories and rumors about the new super flu, but nobody had seen it like this, it made the situation hit home. Some broke out in tears, some with weak stomachs fought the urge to vomit on the floor, and the rest just shook their heads in disgust.

Up on the station monitors, the newscaster blathered on about the outbreak, but it was nothing like the video from Russia. The blonde who read the news was replaced by a checklist of what to do and not to do if one wanted to avoid catching what was now being affectionately called 'Death Angel' (even the news realized how deadly the outbreak was becoming and adopted the moniker). The platform remained silent until the whistle from the MARC echoed throughout the station, snapping everyone back to the reality of their daily grind. Matt stared at the screen a little longer before turning towards the train.

What virus was so bad they had to incinerate a town for? Matt wondered. *And why aren't we hearing about this?*

That was when he heard the first cough emanate from the crowd.

2

Soon, the train settled into the station and the flurry of moving passengers pushed the news to the status of background noise. The passengers arriving in DC quickly scurried off the train and ran to catch the small amount of taxis that circled the station's front, like a pack of sharks that smelled blood in the water. The ones that weren't fast enough would have to settle for the bus or the subway. The last stragglers grabbed their bags and cleared the car doors as Matt stepped inside, grabbing the window seat in row six that he liked. The people from the platform started to make their way onto the train car when a shrill, piercing cry split through the air. People started running around and a commotion started outside the train car. Placing down his briefcase in his seat, Matt turned his head and looked out the window.

At first all he saw was the glare from the lights inside the train car, so he cupped his hands around his eyes. He saw much better with the glare eliminated. To his amazement, there were about ten men holding down what appeared to be a six or seven year old girl. Her frizzy hair and clothes were covered in what appeared to be raspberry jam. Matt scanned around the crowd and saw one of the men holding his hand wrapped in the bottom of his shirt. The shirt's light yellow blossomed red as he continued as his hand bled into it. Someone came over to him and looked at his hand. When Matt saw the wound, he turned his head away, forcing the rising bile back down his throat.

Regaining his composure, he peeked back out the window. The man's pointer and middle finger were bitten off and bits of skin hung down. The gleaming white of bone shone through where the digits got ripped from the hand. The man shook and dropped to the ground in convulsions, slipping into shock. Another man jumped in and quickly lifted the bleeding man's head and placed the man's wallet in his mouth so he wouldn't bite his tongue off.

While everyone's attention was on the man, the little girl bit another one of the hands holding her down. Her teeth dug into the meat on the back of the man's hand and when she pulled back, his flesh ripped apart, splashing her face in a spray of blood. The others who held her quickly released her in surprise and she spun to the ground. She looked up at the train car and locked eyes with Matt. He found himself staring into two inky pools, swirling around within her eye sockets. She swung her head away and springing to her feet, ran into the crowd, disappearing into the wave of people flooding into the station.

Matt sat and watched, horrified by the grisly scene. The station emergency crew rushed onto the platform and started working on the two wounded men. The crowd gathered closer around them, but then started to dissipate when just like in the internet video clip, three men in biohazard suits made their way through the crowd toward the chaotic scene.

They surrounded the injured men and quickly set up a clear plastic tent around them. Two more people in biohazard suits rushed onto the platform wheeling gurneys in front of them. Once they set a perimeter, they put the men on the gurneys and strapped them down. Matt could see them talk into their walkie-talkies and inject the men with syringes.

"Weird shit out there man," said the grungy looking teen as he sat down next to Matt. Matt turned to the person invading his personal space and managed a weak smile when he noticed it was the guy with the iPhone from earlier. The kid wore a faded Nirvana tee shirt and ripped jeans. He had straggly brown hair that an old trucker hat tried in vain to contain underneath.

"I don't know what the hell is going out there. Did you see the girl bite them?" asked Matt.

"Yeah man, I was about to get on the train when I heard that dude scream. I've never heard anyone scream like that," His voice lowered to a whisper as he finished his sentence, "I wonder how the suits knew to get here so fast. It's like they were already here."

Matt turned his head around to look back outside the window. The scene was being cleared and now there were

Baltimore police clearing the station. The conductor and the engineer both stood at the front of the train and waited patiently to see if the train could leave. They both looked over and waved to the security office, which was about fifty feet from the platform. Matt sighed in relief as they boarded and he could hear the train start to power up.

"Maybe I won't be as late as I thought," he mumbled to himself.

The teen turned back to him, pulling an earbud out, "What'd you say?"

"Nothing, just glad we are getting this thing going, that's all." He glanced at his Rolex and put his hand underneath his jacket and briefcase. He wasn't sure if he could trust the kid next to him not to mug him when they disembarked later in Baltimore. He stood six-three and weighed two twenty, but that didn't mean he wanted to fight the guy.

Matt felt the train lurch forward and relaxed as they started leaving the station. He heard three people cough in unison as he checked his watch again, thinking about how late he was going to be.

3

Matt dozed off ten minutes after the train departed the station. He stayed up late all weekend working on a project for the consulting firm he worked for. His supervisor never told him what he was working on, but he knew he had to create a containment system for cities in the event of some un-named catastrophe for the DHS and CDC. He based his project on a dirty-bomb scenario since that seemed to be the only act of terrorism nobody had any idea about how to contain. He finished the ground work for a containment field created by sound waves. The waves vibrated at such a high velocity and density that the fallout wouldn't spread to other adjacent areas. The science was sketchy, but he needed to show them something to keep the earmarks from Congress flowing in. He only came up with the ideas; he didn't have to build them. Building them was left up to the guys with a higher pay grade, which suited Matt fine.

He napped restlessly. In his mind he saw the girl again. He looked down at her questioningly while she ate a severed hand. Her lips smacked together and he could hear the flesh rip from the appendage as the girl chewed on it like she hadn't eaten in weeks. She looked up at him with a crimson smile and held the hand up for him to try. Her empty eyes locked onto his gaze and he realized her eyes were like staring into the abyss. She smiled and opened her arms to him, beckoning him to hold her. Unconsciously, Matt started to rub the place on his leg where is nephew bit him two days ago as the girl held him in his dream.

Matt was still sleeping and touching the mark on his leg when the train came to a sudden halt. He slowly brought himself from the depths of sleep and grabbed his briefcase ready to go when he looked outside the window. They were sitting in the middle of nowhere. Trees surrounded them on the left and a field of tall grass on the right. The other passengers on the car started to stir and stare out the windows.

"What the fuck is this?" yelled a man in Washington Bullets jersey. "Where the fuck are we? This don't look like no damn Baltimore!"

All over the car, people began voicing their extreme displeasure with the sudden stop. The speakers in the ceiling crackled as the engineer came on.

"Attention all passengers, we have been ordered to stop the train and await clearance to enter the Baltimore area. We are about half way in between the DC metro area and Baltimore. Everyone please remain calm and we should be moving again shortly. Thank you and sorry for any inconvenience this might have caused," the speaker crackled again into silence.

A yell of, "Inconvenience my ass!" echoed through the car and some people nervously laughed.

Murmurs started to flood the car. Matt picked out bits and pieces of conversations and complaints while they looked for information on their phones. He really couldn't have cared less, but he was due to present to some DHS and CDC heavy weights in a few hours at the office. Checking his cell phone, he found there was still no service. The rest of the passengers started finding out they couldn't get a signal either and the murmurs grew louder.

A loud crash sounded from the car's front. Two people seated upfront shot up out of their seats and went to the door that connects to the next car. They screamed when they looked through the window into the other the car. Matt jumped out of his seat and almost tripped over the grungy kid from earlier as he tried to get to the front and take a peek. Matt pushed his way to the door and stopped dead when he surveyed the other car. All he saw was a red painted window. The screams inside the other car were shrill and full of terror, and then they were silenced. He only heard some grunting and a sound like someone tearing cloth. Then the wet smacking sounds began. He brought his hand up to his mouth as he tried to block the bile that came flooding up his throat and burned in his mouth. Then something else happened and Matt's blood ran cold.

For the first time Matt coughed and tiny crimson droplets dotted his hand.

4

The train sat idle for over an hour with no updates from the conductor. The cell phones were still silent. The twelve riders on car number four all took turns listening to the car in front of them to figure out what happened. The sounds diminished to silence and there were no other signs of life. A couple of men, including the one with the Bullets jersey, decided to try the car behind them. They peered through the two sets of glass doors and saw that nothing unusual was going on. They came back to the front and had a seat.

"So what exactly the fuck is going on around here? The train's been stopped and the next car looks like somebody threw red paint all over the door," said the Bullet man. When he finished, he placed his head in his hands and rested them on his knees.

They sat in silence for a while. Boredom set in so Matt decided to strike up a conversation. Standing up, he let out another cough and said, "I think we should get to know each other better, we might be here awhile. I'm Matt Thomas and I only want to get to work on time."

Bullet spoke up next, "Um, Vernon James and I only want to get to my son. He lives with his mom in Baltimore and I was picking him up so we could spend the week together."

"My name's Zach White and I just wanted to get to my girlfriend's house," said the teen who had sat next to Matt earlier.

More coughs echoed through the train car. Everyone glanced around to take note of who coughed. The ones who did quickly put their hands down on their laps and pretended nothing happened.

A shrill cry sounded out from the back of the car. Matt and several others shot to their feet and ran to the back. In the rear seats, they found a man hunched over and not breathing. An old woman shook him on the shoulder, crying out his name as she did.

"Robert! Robert, wake up!"

Zach reached over and gently patted her back. "Excuse me," he said in a light tone. The woman almost didn't hear him.

"Please help him, he's not breathing!"

One of the men who rushed back to help, dropped to his knees and felt for a pulse.

"I'm a doctor, let me check him out," he said as he checked Robert's body.

"Has he been sick lately?"

"Not really. Why?"

"He feels really hot and his skin is clammy."

"Well, he's been coughing a lot the last two days."

The doctor started to examine the man's body. He found nothing out of the ordinary on his head and face. His arms and hands were also clear of anything. Finally he felt for a pulse and found nothing when he placed his fingers over the man's wrist.

"I'm sorry ma'am. Saying 'sorry for your loss' just sounds too cliché to me," he said quietly as he closed Robert's eyelids.

The woman threw herself onto her dead husband and sobbed loudly.

The doctor turned to Vernon, "Will you please escort her away for now."

After Vernon lead the woman a couple of rows away, the doctor bent down lower and pulled up Robert's pant leg. The doctor flinched back in surprise. Beneath the skin, just above the sock line, a dark shape darted up the leg under the skin.

"Bingo," he whispered to himself as he swiftly stood back up.

"Bingo what?" asked Matt.

"He has a bite mark on his left ankle that is consistent with what we have been hearing about those with the Death Angel virus. They all seem to exhibit some sort of bite that introduced the virus into the system. We have been trying to figure out if the virus only spreads through salvia from the bite, or any other bodily fluid. I can assure you it is not airborne or we would all be infected now. Vernon, you can let the woman come back to her husband now."

"So how do you know so much?" asked Zach as he, Matt, and the doctor moved away from the back of the car.

"Name's Kurt Johnson, CDC. The reports of a patient zero surfaced only a few weeks ago and we've been trying to play catch up ever since," he answered as he got out his phone and quickly tried to send a text message. The message failed. Kurt sighed and put his phone back in his pocket.

"What the hell do you mean 'catch up'?" asked Zach.

"I meant it in a 'that is all I'm at liberty to say' way," Kurt retorted.

Matt rubbed his forehead and the light heat of a slight fever welcomed him. He quickly put his arms down and looked to make sure nobody saw him. When he looked at his arms, he swore he saw something move just below his skin. Blinking, he glanced down again and didn't see it. The doctor glanced in his direction and then turned away again.

Matt decided to get the conversation going again and change the subject, "So, I'm Matt, he's Zach, and the guy over there is Vernon, so who are the rest of you guys? We might as well get acquainted in case we're here for a while."

A man in a three piece suit stood up and spoke, "I'm Donald Fuchs. I work as a day trader for J.P. Morgan's Baltimore office." Feeling his duty was done, he sat back down and pulled his Wall Street Journal back out and stuck his nose in it again. He buried his face in the pages when he flew into a coughing fit. When he brought the paper back down, he wiped the blood from the corner of mouth with the back of his hand. Donald looked down at it and quickly pulled his coat over his hands to hide it from the rest of the passengers.

The woman in the back hunched over the body of her dead husband rose and wiped the tears from her eyes on her sleeve. Regaining her composure, she cleared her throat. "I'm Jane Clark," she said in between sniffles, "and my husband is... was Robert. We were ju... just on vacation to see our daughter who goes to school at Georgetown. He only wanted to go into Baltimore while we were here to see the... the...

Orioles play a game." Jane began crying again and threw herself over her husband's corpse.

The last mystery rider stood up in the front of the car. The tall, blond man was dressed in sweatpants and a tee shirt that stretched over his bulging muscles. He pulled his shirt up and hanging from his waistband was a gold badge.

"John Killian, U.S. Marshall Service." He picked a duffel bag up out of the seat and unzipped it. John pulled two Glocks and a shoulder harness out of the bag and proceeded to put them on. "I'm on the train as random security. These might come in handy if what happened on the other car happens here," he said checking the clips on the pistols.

On cue a loud thumping sounded out from the car in front of them. John stood with his back to the door and the sudden thud caused to him to jump. He turned in a fluid motion, drawing his gun, pointing it at the door. The blood covering the other car's window blocked their view, keeping them from looking in. The banging continued growing louder and louder until the glass shattered. Four arms reached through the gaping hole, hands grasping at the empty air. The glass shards pierced the arms and a dark ichor oozed from the wounds. In the act of being forced through the window, some skin got cleaved off one arm and hung down until the weight of it pulled it to the floor. It landed with a wet splash. The metal door locks started to groan as the bodies pushed and slammed into the door. Then with a hiss of air, the door gave way.

Vernon stared at the flailing appendages pushing through the door with his mouth agape. "Holy shit," he muttered before he dove down behind the seat he was closest to.

Matt, Zach, and John started to look around for anything they could use to block the door. Frantically, they tugged and pulled on the seats and grabbing luggage stacked it in front of the door. Zach pulled a hand rail free and used it to brace seats and baggage barricading the doorway.

"Shit! Quick, get to the back!" John yelled as the first thuds from the fists hitting the door echoed throughout the car.

The three turned toward the back and froze. Kneeling there, dripping crimson was Robert. Donald and Kurt were on the floor sliding under the seats toward the front and stood when they reached the others. Huddled together, they stared in disbelief at Robert. His face was smeared with blood and in his mouth he chewed on an ear he had ripped from his wife Jane's head. Her bloody body lay beside him. Matt looked and realized why they never heard a cry or a struggle. Her head lay at an odd, un-natural angle. Robert broke her neck and then proceeded to consume her while they focused on the commotion in the front. Her arms were covered with weeping bite wounds covering her flesh. The blood pooled under her and slowly started to run down the center aisle of the train car toward Donald and Kurt.

"John, can I use one of those?" Matt asked as he pointed to one of the Glocks in John's hands.

They both looked as the luggage and seat barrier gave way where the others battered and pushed against it. Zach looked and vomited when he noticed the barrier was being beaten down with the torso of a person. The wet slamming sounds of raw meat and blood hitting the seats filled the train car. The group in the middle looked back and forth from

Robert's feast on his wife to the four that were now entering through the front of the car.

"Yeah, you can. Are you a good shot?" John answered as he handed the gun to Matt.

"Never shot one in my life," Matt said as he looked at the gun in his hand and sighed. He always tried to live a nice, quiet, and peaceful existence so the idea of him now totting a gun seemed ludicrous to him. He stood there, staring down at the loaded weapon in his hands.

"Matt, you ok? Safety is off already so just point and shoot," John instructed as he turned so that him and Matt were back to back, "you take Robert and I'll take the other four in the front."

Both men raised their Glocks in the air, aiming to their respective targets. Vernon, Zach, and Kurt ducked into the seats on either side of John and Matt.

Matt kept his gun pointed down at Robert, who had gone back to eating Jane's face on the floor. The stinging stomach acid rose in the back of his throat again as he watched her being devoured. He jumped when the shot rang out from John's gun. The roar from the guns created a deafening crash in the close confines. Matt felt his ears pop and the car around him fell silent as the ringing pulsed through is head. He watched the movement in the car go into slow motion like a movie playing out before him. He turned to see one of the gore covered people fall in a bloody haze. John fired three more shots and dropped the others where they stood. The acid stench of gunpowder mixed with the cooper twang of blood. Matt and John looked on as the remains of the four intruders slid down what remained of the front door.

The noise in the car made Robert look up from his meal. No longer preoccupied, he threw his half eaten wife aside and started getting up. The moist shuffle of feet through the blood soaked floor alerted Matt to Robert's advance. He brought the gun to bear fast because Robert moved on him quick, quicker than he thought a corpse could move. Robert brought his hands up to latch on to Matt and he stopped, sniffed the air around Matt and turned back around suddenly disinterested in Matt as a meal. The hesitation allowed John to act. He sprung over Matt, pushing him down and firing in one fluid motion. The bullet found its mark and Robert's head exploded, showering grey matter, bone, and a scarlet rain on the back of the train car. Silence filled the car as Matt and John stood in the smoke. Matt looked down at his gun and wondered why he didn't fire at Robert. He tried, but his finger never squeezed the trigger, refusing to do what he wanted his finger to do.

"Where's Donald?" asked Vernon as he started to slide on belly out into the aisle.

"Oh shit," answered Zach. He looked directly into Donald's blank eyes. He didn't blink or breathe. He waved his hand in front of Donald's face and still got no reaction. Slowly, Zach backed out from under the seat and stood back up in the aisle. When Zach turned his head and found himself looking down the barrel of John's gun.

John lowered the gun from Zach's nose, "What?"

"Donald's dead too and I thought I would be safer up here until I got a face full of gun," Zach said as he brushed the dirt from the floor off his jacket.

"Let me see," said Vernon as he got on his hands and knees next to Donald.

An ear splitting scream echoed through the car. Everyone turned to Vernon and gasped. Vernon screamed again as Donald's teeth tore into his neck and reared back. Blood sprayed out from the wound and torn flesh flew through the air as Donald swung his head around. He gulped down the morsel and buried his bloody face back into Vernon.

Vernon flinched in shock, but his arms just hung at his sides and he made no attempt to get away. Gore poured down Vernon's front as it flowed like a river down his Bullet's jersey. Robert stopped slurping the blood from Vernon's throat and dropped his body on the floor. Vernon hit like a sack of potatoes and lay unmoving in the pool of his blood. Donald looked at the rest of the group, his smile red with small chunks of meat stuck between his teeth. Matt noticed the swift movements beneath Donald's skin and looked into his eyes. They too had turned into inky pools.

John quickly brought his gun up and fired a shot. The flames jumped from the muzzle and the shot was deafening in the small train compartment. The bullet caught Donald in his arm and spun him around from the force of the impact. He turned back toward John and the grisly smile was gone, replaced instead by the look of utter, unbridled rage. This time John noticed the black clouds of Donald's eyes too. They shone back at him like black holes, absorbing and destroying the light. He started to stumble at John, but this time John's aim was true. The second shot crashed into Donald's forehead and the back of his head disappeared in a pink spray. Gore, brain, and bone fragments showered the back window. The black faded from Donald's eyes and his body fell to the floor.

"What the hell was that?" Zach yelled out to nobody in particular.

"That is what the Death Angel does to an infected person. The virus pools with more of itself and forms those worm like things you saw writhing underneath the skin," Kurt said as he crawled out from his hiding spot.

"Wow that would have been nice to know before now. Anything else we should know?" Zach said in a wiseass tone.

Matt cleared his throat and coughed again, "Is that why the news is covering up what the Russians were doing to the infected villages? They know YouTube can't be seen as the most trusted news source around."

"Since the Cold War, there is a standing order for the U.S. transportation system, in the event of a contagion breakout, to help contain any infection. D.C. could be quantized now, explaining why were stopped on the tracks. They could be trying to keep the outbreak from spreading to Baltimore," John said, reloading his gun. "The outbreak must have grown large enough to trigger the protocols."

"I strongly suggest we take care of Jane and Vernon before they come back," Kurt said kneeling down to examine Vernon's corpse. He lifted Vernon's eyelids and watched as the black started to coalesce in his pupils. "We'd better do it quickly. The virus is slow to react with the corpse if it has just infected a body, but this is behaving as if the virus was already in his system."

"I like the sound of that," John answered as he walked to the back and aiming the gun at Jane's head, pulled the trigger. Vernon's body was next.

"What I don't get is why did Robert hesitate when he came at you, Matt?" Kurt pondered as he got back to his feet. The blood that splashed on his face from John shooting

Vernon ran down to the corner of his lips. In an involuntary response, he licked his lips. The coopery taste filled his mouth and he gasped, realizing what he just did. He could already feel the virus collect in his system and he welcomed it.

"I don't know!" Matt shouted and laid his gun down on the nearest seat. "I don't fucking know!" he shouted again as John moved closer to him.

"I think I know why," John muttered quietly. He started to tighten his grip on the gun. Matt turned his head to look at Kurt and felt the thing infecting him swim under his skin, invading his body. He started to turn to Kurt for some sort of help when the gunshot next to his ear deafened him. John fell backwards and slammed up against a seat. A growing red spot appeared in John's chest and he dropped to his knees. He looked up at Kurt still pointing the gun Matt had sat down next to him.

"And I know why," Kurt said shaking his head. He pulled the trigger again and John's stomach burst open from the large caliber bullet, spilling his intestines onto the floor. The life faded from his eyes and he fell into the seat beside him.

"Let's have a seat and let's just go to sleep Matt," Kurt suggested.

Matt sat down in his seat and propped his head up against the cool window. He could feel the contagion's tightening grip and coughed. The cool glass felt good on his increasingly hot flesh. Kurt came over and sat down beside him. They gave each other a knowing nod, connected in their new brotherhood. They felt the train car lurch a little as Kurt turned the gun towards his self and pulled the trigger into his chest.

Meanwhile up at the controls, the engineer who died two hours ago from his contact with virus at the station three days ago began stirring again. The train's automated system activated and the engine roared back to life. After a few minutes, the train began moving toward Baltimore again, Matt slept and Kurt buried his head in his hands, weeping loudly in the otherwise silent train car, realizing he couldn't take it all back. He looked down at the blood seeping from his wound and tried to make peace with himself.

In the back, Zach stayed silent, hoped they didn't know he was still alive, and for the first time in his life he prayed.

5

Nathan Pike stood on the loading platform and clinched his fist in rage. The trains were really late and he was going to be late for his son's play. Ten minutes here or there was typical when he dealt with public transportation, but Nathan thought four hours was a little excessive. Over two hours of excuses wore on his last nerve; it wasn't like he had any other options. It was the train or walking. It never failed that shit like this always happened when he was in a hurry and it greatly annoyed him to no end. The intercom sounded about an hour ago and gave some bullshit announcement that there was a mechanical problem with the train. It didn't make a difference to him though; the train was an hour late already. To his relief and amazement, Nathan finally heard the tracks rumble and relaxed slightly. He made his way over to the loading area and waited.

The train crept in and came to a complete stop at the platform. A car down from where Nathan was standing, a woman screamed in horror as she was the first to see the blood splattered windows. He didn't pay attention as he geared himself up to rush on. He heard the airbrakes' decompressing hiss and the doors whoosh open. Without waiting for the doors to totally open, Nathan quickly hopped up to the door and got on the first boarding stair when something stopped him in his tracks. His foot slipped in a thick liquid on the first step. Looking up he saw blood and bits of meat were on the stairs in front of him. He heard a grunt next to him and snapped his head around to see what caused the guttural noise. Someone yelled from the back door and then ran wildly into the station.

Nathan stared up at two men hunched over a bloody body. They were covered in crimson, their faces buried in the body on the floor. Both turned their heads towards Nathan and smiled candy apple smiles. Reaching out, the two corpses grabbed him and ripped into his arms. Nathan stared at their empty obsidian eyes and screamed again when the black moved through their irises like a wave. He felt something push into his arm through the bite marks, burning while it started to move through him. Every move they made through his body grew increasingly more painful.

At last, the jabbing sensation he felt in the base of his skull made Nathan realize he would never make it to his son's play.

***

STORY NOTES:

One of my goals is write a screenplay for something I've written and I think that cinematic vision crept into my head when I wrote this. Honestly, as much as I've tried to not write about zombies, they keep creeping back up in my work. This is also one of my favorite pieces. In most stories we see the aftermath or the beginnings of the zombie plague on a broad scale. We see the large cities being over-run or the mass chaos being fueled by a hysteric media. Sitting back to write this I wanted to remove the information flooding the media and place the characters in an isolated setting while they witness the plague take hold around them. Why a train? I used a train because I could place the cast in a small space in the middle of nowhere and let the situation play out without any outside interference. Like I stated earlier, I also wrote this one like a movie in my head and the few sets made sense for me if it were to become a short film. I'm only lending a hand to anybody to would want to film it…

ABOUT BRENT ABELL

Brent Abell resides in Southern Indiana with his wife, sons, and a pug who is worshiped as a minor deity in some religions. His work has been featured in multiple anthologies and eZines. His first novella, *In Memoriam,* was released in 2013 and he has completed his first full novel. He is currently working on his next novel, novella, and trying to get through the heap of story ideas floating around on his desk. You can keep up with all the latest news at:

http://brentabell.wordpress.com

APPENDIX: FIRST PUBLISHING CREDITS

Tears of Heaven - First published in *From Beyond the Grave,* Grinning Skull Press, 2013

Spot Shoot - First published in *New Dawn Fades,* Post Mortem Press, 2011

Giver - First published in *The Sirens Call #12,* Sirens Call Publications, 2013

As I Crossed Lincoln Bridge - First published in *Father Grim's Storybook,* Wicked East Press, 2012

Winds of War - First published in *Horrific History,* Hazardous Press, 2013

The Heart's Longing - Original to this collection

Calvary Hill - First published in *Under the Stairs,* Wicked East Press, 2011

Do Us Part - First published in *The Sirens Call #8,* Sirens Call Publications. 2013

The Sleeper Wakes - First published in *Pavor Nocturnus Dark Fiction Anthology Vol. 1,* Parasomnia Press, 2013

For Our Sins: A Fable - First published in *Ten Silver Bullets,* Crowded Quarantine Press, 2012

Midnight Rider - First published in *Coffin Hop: Death by Drive-In!,* Coffin Hop Press, 2013

Those Last Minutes - Original to this collection

The Conversation - First published in *Daily Flash: 366 Days of Flash Fiction Leap Year Edition,* Pill Hill Press, 2011

Rivals - First published in *Short Sips: Coffee House Flash Fiction V.2,* Wicked East Press, 2011

Beneath - Original to this collection

The Becoming - First published in *Surreal Grotesque eZine Vol.9,* 2013 and *The Sirens Call eZine #16,* Sirens Call Publications, 2014

Sweet Nothings - Original to this collection

The Reaper Rides - First published in *Undead Tales 2,* Rymfire Undead, 2012

ALSO BY BRENT ABELL

Now Available

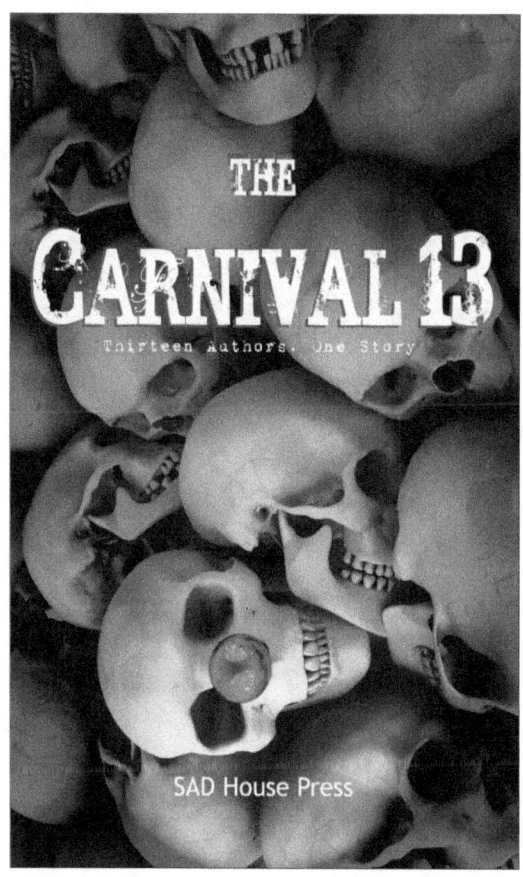

A 13 Author Round-Robin Experience…

All Proceeds Donated to Scares That Care!

www.ingramcontent.com/pod-product-compliance
Lightning Source LLC
Chambersburg PA
CBHW060131130626
46556CB00006B/2312